The Cursed Garden

An Enchanted Forest Novel

ALICIA J. CHUMNEY

Cover Design: Jennifer Ayres
1. Fantasy 2. Retold Fairy Tale 3. Novella
First Edition

Table of Contents

Prologue

Tradition

Nobody thought anything about heirs when Queen Gabrielle of Wonderland had a daughter first. In fact, they celebrated long into the night. Princess Alice the Sixth made her appearance screaming her lungs out until one of her cousins, a Diamond, leaned over her crib and smiled. From that moment the cousins formed a bond and were nearly inseparable playmates while growing up despite the three year age difference.

Two years later Grace surprised everybody when she made her quiet appearance into the world. Everybody was expecting a little prince to make his grand appearance and instead they started researching family trees and Traditions.

This little princess bonded almost instantly with one of her non-Jack cousins. It should have been the first sign that things weren't going to go Traditionally.

Two more years after that Nadine made her blinking appearance. The Queen was beginning to ever despair of having her son, but the lands were still prospering and

four-year-old Alice was now too old to be sent off to be
fostered.

Nobody ever expected the Queen to send her children
off after the various edicts she had made over the years.
Only the welfare of Wonderland could ever convince her
otherwise.

It wasn't until their fourth child, a son named Charlie,
appeared that people began to take notice of the changes
that were occurring to Wonderland.

The King balefully pointed out that their four children
– an unheard of number in the Wonderland genealogy –
may have been because of his family's line.

Traditions were looked over with a fine toothcomb as
they began to prepare for what was to happen, only
nobody knew what was about to come. And people began
to notice that Wonderland was beginning to flounder.
Harvests were starting to fail. Plants would refuse to
grow. Singing Flowers lost their melodic harmonies and
began crooning off-key. Growth Mushrooms shrunk
people and Shrinking Mushrooms grew people. A chaos
unlike the controlled chaos that had been carefully
cultivated throughout generations had begun to take root in
Wonderland!

Henry the Heart and Stephan the Spade began looking
at their own children for a child that was the right age.
They both knew what was about to happen. Derek
released his breath knowing that his own four were too old
for the task that was soon to be necessary. The Queen,
holding her infant son in one arm and her toddler daughter

in the other, began to cry as she realized that Wonderland would not give her a choice on fostering. "When I was with the Harringtons I had a cousin..."

And with those fateful words, Nadine Lorie Jackson was sent off to be fostered. Her mother's bodyguard – the Spade – was the one to provide Nadine's Tracker.

Nobody ever expected that they would lose Nadine.

Part One

Chapter 1

The Book

The woods were dense around the house that no longer looked like a mere house. The house she swore she would never step foot in again. It was a fruitless promise to herself. *He* was the only person who could help her. *He* was the only person who knew what to do. *He* was the only person who had haunted her dreams for the past thirteen years.

"Let me in!" she shouted, pounding on the doors and praying that he was home. "I need your help!" Everything around her was dark. B*ut it is late*, she reasoned. He would have to allow the crazy girl banging on the windows in the house, wouldn't he? "Please," she began to sob, looking behind her at the gate she had entered, hoping that they did not know where she went. "I need you."

From the shadows of the garden, he had watched her frantic run down the drive, through the gate, and up to the entryway of his house. Its glamour was beginning to fade away and soon the façade of a normal house would return to its original castle form. He did not move until her sobbing had left her leaning against the door, immobile.

She did not see him approach her, barely felt him picking her up and taking her inside. His heat warmed her chilled body and the tears kept pouring out of her as her tense muscles relaxed slightly from his warmth and the fact that she now knew that he would help her. "I'm sorry. I know I promised to never come back."

"It's okay," he mumbled, managing to lock the door behind them. He knew that she had no choice in the matter. That was the trouble with The Tradition. "Tell me what happened."

"Guy found the book," she whispered before passing out from exhaustion and relief.

A few hours later, finding herself curled up on a bed, Nadine jerked upright and frantically looked around the room before the memory of her race to find Richmond and tell him about the theft of the book. The very book that she had been guarding since she was eight and had stumbled on the then twelve-year-old boy.

"It's okay," Richmond comforted her from where he had resumed hiding in the shadows. "The book was meant to be stolen."

"You could have told me *that* thirteen years ago!" she mumbled, looking for her red hoodie. "Where is…"

"It's put away." Still standing in the shadows, "Do you know the significance of that book?"

"It was just a book of fairy tales." She started to stand up but found herself still too tired to move. She wondered if Guy had found where she had left her car at the head of the trail leading to the house in the woods.

Only it wasn't really a house anymore, was it?

"And do you know which tale you are currently in?"

Nadine sat up, her eyes wide.

"Once upon a time," eight-year-old Nadine Witt read aloud from the book she had been given by the boy in the woods, "lived a frog. He wasn't just an ordinary frog; he was a handsome prince who had been transformed into a frog and…" she looked up. "A lot of these stories have somebody being transformed into something else." Shutting the book with a snap, she put it back in the special box hidden under the bed and closed her eyes.

She remembered Richmond claiming that he had been frozen in time, at the age of twelve, for more years than he cared to remember until she had stumbled on his house. 'That's silly,' she had laughed at the time. 'That only happens in fairy tales.' Without a word, Richmond disappeared and then returned with a book. 'Then maybe you need to start believing in fairy tales,' he whispered, handing over the book and disappearing back into his house.

It had looked a lot like a cottage that was found between the pages of the book in front of her. It had been abandoned, except for Richmond, and there were red roses everywhere in the middle of the woods. She could have sworn she had passed the very spot where the trail leading to his house had appeared at least a million times with her father while they went fishing.

"Ribbit," a frog croaked from the open window of her room. Looking back and forth from the frog and the box, Nadine's eyes flew open. The front page of the book had read, "Be careful what you read aloud." Taking a hop, the frog croaked again, "Ribbit."

"I'm supposed to kiss you, aren't I?" Nadine squeaked, mostly from fear of what would happen.

"Ribbit."

She didn't want to get the book back out to check, but the versions she had heard were pretty clear, she had to kiss the frog.

Picking him up, she squished her eyes closed, puckered her lips, and kissed the frog's head. Peeking between squinted eyes, she did not see any clouds of smoke or a Prince. Opening her eyes, the frog still rested in her hands. "Ribbit."

Laughing, "I guess I allowed my imagination to get the best of me." She paused for a second. "That's what Heather always tells me," she said to the frog.

Disappointed, the Frog Prince hopped away in search of somebody who had read the tale where he had to be thrown against the wall and not kissed.

"That was real?" She blinked. "But I kissed that frog and nothing happened."

Richmond laughed, "You never finished reading that tale. In the original story, the frog was thrown against the wall." Leaning against the wall, the shadows hiding him even further, he added, "And a few other tales have gone unfinished because you never read the book aloud completely. In some instances that is a good thing."

Nadine's eyes widened. "It all started that day I was lost in the woods and found you."

"Hansel and Gretel, minus Hansel," he added.

She added, "The Frog Prince."

"Cinderella," Richmond retorted.

Slowly she whispered, "Little Red Riding Hood." Nadine's head jerked at that tale, thinking of the red hoodie she favored. "Are you the wolf then?"

Drawing a deep breath, Richmond relied on knowledge he knew by magical means. "No. Guy was until you escaped him."

Closing her eyes as if she dreaded the answer, "Then what tale am I currently living in?"

"Beauty and the Beast." Stepping out of the shadows, he let her see his bearded face. It was a drastic change from the young boy he once was and the man he was today. The new addition, the part that let him know that Nadine was soon to arrive, were the claws where his hands should have been. "This will be your last tale since Guy stole the book from under your bed."

Holding back her shriek of surprise, Nadine felt the mantle of Tradition falling over her. Now she believed that the tales in that book, and probably others, were real.

Chapter 2

The Woods

- Thirteen Years Before -

Allen Wit felt a pull towards Heather Monroe and her twin children from the very moment he met them.

It wasn't love at first sight; that he'd shared with his first wife, Lindsey Harrington. It barely even came close, emotionally, to the heartbreak they felt when they realized that Lindsey couldn't have children. It didn't even touch what he felt when Lindsey's cousin, Gabrielle asked them to adopt her daughter for reasons that were never clear to him.

However, he was still drawn to her as if by magic. He could see himself practicing ball with her ten-year-old son, Matt. Eight-year-old Nadine would have an older sister to play with in Meg.

That would all change with one fateful camping trip.

For Nadine, it was supposed to be a simple camping trip with her father, stepmother, and twin stepsiblings. She loved camping with her father and it would be the first time they'd gone camping with the others. She couldn't wait to share the experience of the hiking trails, fishing, and roasting marshmallows over the campfire for s'mores.

Regrettably, the stepsiblings moaned and complained about every little thing including the lack of a bathroom and no internet. For people who were supposed to be ten they certainly acted like they were six. They just had to last one more night.

If asked later Nadine would not be able to recall how she had ended up alone in the woods. Up until that moment, she would have sworn that Heather cared about her just as much as the twins.

"Honey," Heather's silky voice had purred, something that had amazed herself at the time. "I think we ran out of bread." She had looked everywhere for the bread she thought remained in the bag, at least half a loaf, but it had gone missing.

Allen stood up and searched his pockets for his keys. "I'll run to that convenience store we passed coming in and pick some up."

"I'll go with you," Nadine had hopped up.

"No, stay here and help Heather," and with that her father was gone for at least an hour.

Ten minutes later, Heather spoke up again with a confused expression on her face "It seems we are out of firewood. Matt, Meg, go find some."

"Do I have to?" Matt whined.

Meg pouted, "I don't wanna."

Nadine spoke up without intending too and blurted out, "I'll do it!" Taking a step backward, she wondered why she had volunteered; she hated collecting firewood. The bark and branches scratched, and on occasion, actually cut her. She was also allergic to poison ivy and firewood hunting off the beaten trails was a sure-fire way for her to come in contact with the plant.

And with those fateful three words, eight-year-old Nadine was left to wander the woods looking for firewood.

Without realizing it, she stepped off the trail. It wasn't until several minutes had passed that Nadine noticed what she had done. Making matters worse, she began to turn in circles looking for any evidence of the path. It had vanished. The workings of a magic forest in the real world were unexpected and it didn't occur to her that she was being forced into a fairy tale. Fairy tales weren't real. They didn't exist outside of the bedtime stories her mother had insisted on telling her.

Instead, the trees seemed to close up around her. For a moment it appeared that the sky had darkened. Taking ten steps back into the direction Nadine thought the campsite was at was enough for her to find a trail on the other side of a fallen tree trunk.

The trail existed. She had gone camping with her father for years before he had married Heather. They frequently walked this trail to go fishing to catch their dinner. That was until Meg whined about the fish being slimy and Matt made enough noise to scare every living animal in the forest away.

She doubted that there would be any more camping trips in their future.

Grabbing her small stack of sticks, she cautiously walked down the trail, hoping that she was going in the right direction. Not a minute later, the sky lightened and Nadine found herself at the gates of a massive rose garden. Exiting the woods, she could barely see the house in the middle of all of the roses.

Pushing open the gates and wincing when the rusted hinges protested, Nadine entered the garden. She stumbled as the manor house surrounded by roses came into view. The house was dark and dirty with its broken and filthy windows, ivy of a dubious nature covering one side, stone bricks that looked as if they were perilously close to falling out of the walls, and a thick coat of fallen leaves covering everything else. In contrast, perfect pink buds, sunny yellow blossoms, radiant red blooms, and blemish-free white petals blended in dazzlingly with hybrids and roses with many colors in one flower. A boy, a few years older than Nadine, glared darkly at the pint-sized intruder. "Who are you and what are you doing here?"

Gulping, "My name is Nadine and I got lost in the woods looking for firewood." Eyes wide, she stared at the boy. Everything else fell away as she studied the chocolate brown eyes that seemed closed off and matching hair that was in desperate need of a haircut. "I thought this was the trail back to my campsite," she whispered.

"What are you staring at?" he growled.

Taking a step back, "You," she simply answered, noticing the book that he was clutching tightly against his chest. "What book is that?"

"It doesn't concern you," the boy once again growled. *Why won't this girl go away?* He tried hard not to look at the one thing that he hoped that she would and yet would not notice. *She isn't even pretty*, he railed at the curse. *Please don't let her see...* his thoughts trailed off when the observant little girl noticed it.

"That's odd," she whispered, taking a step forward. A cloud had shifted, sending a shaft of sunlight directly on what she had thought was merely another yellow rose. Instead, this perfect bloom glittered wickedly, as if trying to catch her attention. "Is that gold?"

"Yes," the boy gruffly answered, mentally cursing his luck that after three hundred years that this was the person meant to break his curse. The other little girls had simply wanted a pink rose.

"It's beautiful." Nadine did not dare touch it for fear of marring its perfection. "Does it feel like a flower?"

"I don't know." Again he growled, this time close enough that Nadine jumped back. "Take this book and leave."

"But I want to know."

"You'll be back," he darkly promised. "Keep this book safe. As soon as it is stolen from you come back here and let me know. Keep it safe as long as possible for both our sakes. At least twenty years." Hoping that by then she would no longer be a gangly child with dishwater blonde hair, Richmond shoved the book at her, he started to turn to go back into the house.

"I don't know how to get back...," she whispered.

Without turning, he pointed, "Follow the trail. It'll lead you back."

Instead of following his directions, Nadine cocked her head sideways and blurted out one of the things she'd been thinking, "How old are you? You sound funny."

"I don't know how old I am," he answered, not looking at her.

"Why not?"

"Because I'm frozen in time."

"That's silly," she laughed. "That only happens in fairy tales."

"Then maybe you need to start believing in fairy tales," he whispered before disappearing back into his house.

Only then did Nadine do as she was told, looking back only once at the golden rose. With a sigh, she stepped onto the trail. After ten steps she looked back only to see nothing but trees. Ten more steps and she could see her step-mother and step-siblings.

"Where have you been?" Heather snapped with worry, pulling her step-daughter towards her into a hug. Allen would have been furious if Nadine had gone missing on her watch.

"I got lost and then I found," she paused, wondering if she should tell the truth, "this book. It was in a box I found in the woods," she lied.

"Must be those pesky geocachers," Heather smiled. Moments later she sent Matt to find some firewood. "Like I should have done in the first place," she was heard mumbling.

Chapter 3

From the Cinders

- About Three Years Before -

The room was her choice; the rafters in the attic walls and ceiling provided plenty of space for her makeshift bookcases and hiding places. Used books acquired from book sales (five to ten dollars for a bag of books was a good deal) and used bookstores became both a form of wallpaper and a chance to escape the constraints of her reality. The doorway and a staircase became a semi-hidden passage into another world. It was a retreat from Matt's constant sports talk and Meg's giggling with her friends about boys.

Sometimes she found herself doing Meg's chores and occasionally Matt's if his college baseball practices ran long. But it never mattered; her father would take her out to get ice cream or a new book whenever he caught her 'helping' out her stepsiblings. He knew exactly how much easier it was to go along with Meg and Matt's begging than it was to get them to do what they were supposed to be doing.

With her hair always in a ponytail and her nose always in a book, Nadine was easily overlooked at school, but she was okay with it. Her grades were impeccable and several schools were offering academic scholarships; her father was proud and that was all that mattered. She had no need to worry about Prom or if the baseball team made it to State. Nadine wanted out and she, and her father, knew that getting into a good school was her only chance to escape Heather's servitude.

They all heard the late-night arguments where Allen Witt and Heather fought bitterly over money, where Heather frequently held Allen hostage with the money she had inherited from her first husband's accident. Everybody knew that, somehow, Allen's Bakery was floundering despite the long lines that snaked outside the door every day.

Nobody could figure out why the bakery was in trouble, but Heather frequently used her financial stability and cash infusions to keep Allen under her thumb.

Smiling while her classmates and their parents were applauding her valedictorian speech, Nadine rejoined the front row where her best friend and salutatorian waited. The rest of their lives were ahead of them; they had made big plans to escape their families and the small town where everybody knew everything about everybody else.

At the end of the ceremony her father raved about her big surprise – she had told nobody about being the top of her class - and the speech, talking about how proud he was of her and how the rest of her life really was at her feet. Getting into his truck, he promised to meet them at home in an hour; he had to get something that he had forgotten at work. They all suspected it was a celebration cake.

Two hours later a police officer delivered the bad news.

The death of Nadine's father had a bigger impact on the family than anybody else expected. All of her plans and ideas were pushed aside as it was revealed that Heather had put a second mortgage on the house and didn't tell Allen. The money that she had frequently held over his head quickly vanished as neither Heather nor Meg curbed their spending habits and there was no additional source of income to help balance out their spending.

Soon all that was left was the bakery and instead of dealing with running it, Heather sold the property without looking for the ownership papers. By the time it was discovered that Nadine owned the bakery, that money had been spent on mortgage payments and more new clothes that sat in the closets unworn.

Whenever it was suggested that they return those unworn clothes, tags and receipts went missing. Whenever the suggestion of taking the clothes to a consignment store arose the clothes themselves would then vanish.

Excuses after excuses were thrown about.

"Yard sales are so tacky!"

"Nobody wants to wear last year's clothes!"

"That's my favorite shirt!" even when the shirt had never been worn and still had the store tags attached.

Slowly Nadine's book collection disappeared onto the shelves of the one used bookstore that would give cash in exchange for books. The appeal of credit beckoned her, but she needed the money more than she needed more books.

And then, the final nail in their coffin, Nadine had to start working at the Bakery that her father had previously owned. The new owner, Allen's former manager, took pity on the eighteen-year-old and hired her on the spot.

The days were long and tiring. School. Homework. Work.

The weekends were longer with their double shifts.

"Nadine!" Heather called from intercom installed in the kitchen. "Meg spilled something all over the floor and now the floor is sticky! Mop it up!"

Rolling her eyes towards the ceiling, Nadine slipped a pencil in the middle of her U.S. History textbook and snapped it shut. "Coming!" she called back as she leaned across her desk to punch the intercom button. Even though there was a floor between them, she didn't dare say that Meg should clean up her own mess. Sometimes she wondered if Heather had installed a listening device in Nadine's room, even though she had never found anything other than the annoying intercom.

Granted, a sticky floor meant that Meg had attempted to clean up whatever it was that she spilled. At least that's what Nadine wanted to believe.

"Hurry up!" Heather called back.

When Nadine finally entered the kitchen, she noticed the pots and pans all over the place. It looked as if Meg had been doing a science experiment that had exploded all over the place, almost. Something had definitely overflowed on the stove. And onto the floor. A glass of orange juice, probably knocked over when the contents on the stove bubbled over, was still dripping onto the floor.

She could hear Meg giggling from the next room. Her stepsister knew about her U.S. History test and the English Composition that was due - thankfully online - the next day. She'd already had a six-hour shift at the diner and had hoped that she could get some studying and writing done and be in bed at a reasonable hour.

"Meg!" Nadine called out.

"I'm late for my shift!" Meg called back, slipping out of the house.

"Meg!" she helplessly called back again. This was going to take hours, hours she didn't have, with all of the scrubbing and mopping that she was going to have to do. That didn't include the dishes that were going to have to be washed because nobody else could bother to do any of the housework.

It was bad enough that her academic scholarships had to be declined because they only paid for tuition and her dorm room with no money for her books and meal plans. University was replaced with Community College; even then she could only afford nine hours a semester at a time.

But when Heather found herself 'unable to function' after the death of her second husband, everything had fallen on the recent high school graduate to make things run smoothly. Nobody had known that Heather had also been siphoning off most of the profits from the bakery and using that money to keep Allen from leaving.

"Nadine!" Heather called from the living room. "Can you vacuum in here when you are finished? There are candy wrappers everywhere!"

Popping her head into the doorway, Nadine also noticed all of the dishes that had not been taken back into the kitchen. "You have got to be kidding me," she whispered.

"What was that?"

"Nothing," Nadine stated, unable to resist the previous urge to roll her eyes a moment longer.

Body cocooned in blankets, Nadine sighed against the screech of her alarm clock. Another Friday morning class followed by a lunchtime waitressing shift awaited her.

Half asleep and doing three things at once, Nadine gave a half-hearted hit at the button and the alarm found itself on the floor instead of turned off, the annoying beep barely registering in Nadine's tired brain beyond its irritating buzz telling her to, "Wake up already!"

Matt had adjusted well, but he already had a few years of college behind him. He finished school early and conveniently forgot that his mother needed help. Meg, on the other hand, still needed to learn how to do the basics and found herself wearing a similar black apron to the one that Nadine was currently trying to find in the pile of dirty clothing in the corner of her room.

A pounding on the floor from Meg beating her ceiling with a broom used for this very purpose followed by a loud, "Wake up and turn off that alarm clock!" made Nadine pause from fixing her ponytail and realize that the alarm had been sounding for five minutes.

"Sorry," Nadine yelled through the floor. She almost added, "It won't happen again," but it was the fifth time in seven days that it had happened and it was bound to happen again.

Meg, content that the alarm was now turned off, rolled back into her bed. She was not a friend of the late shift, even though she often found herself working it. Meg would have requested a swap with Nadine if she didn't dislike working the lunch shift even more. Nadine, for her own part, was up late studying for her U.S. History test and working on the English composition paper. It had been a long night indeed.

"Nadine," Heather's voice carried from the master bedroom, "can you bring me my breakfast?" Heather didn't need to install an intercom in her bedroom when Nadine wasn't in her room; her voice carried well enough from the second-floor bedroom.

'I'm already running late,' almost slipped out, but she knew Heather was not making a request but a demand. "Yes, ma'am," she replied instead.

Looking around the kitchen, she knew that cold cereal and sugary breakfast pastries were not an option. Eggs, bacon, and biscuits were preferred, but Nadine was already pressed for time. It would have to be oatmeal and coffee. Ten minutes later, she was out the door, car keys - Matt's old car that she shared with Meg - , book bag, and waitressing apron in hand, and heading off to work. Maybe today she would get some time to finish her paper;

Ms. Marge could be very understanding about schoolwork sometimes.

There were no illusions, there would be no rich Prince Charming to rescue her like in the fairy tale book that strange boy had given her ten years ago. She rarely even thought about that camping trip; the sudden memory almost made her over-fill a cup of coffee.

But he would be around twenty-one or twenty-two now, her traitorous head thought. She had sworn never to think about that strange boy in the woods again. *Although you never knew just how old he was, you just assumed that he was eleven or twelve*, her brain persisted on thinking, ignoring the fact that she needed to focus on getting her orders correct.

"Nadine?" Ms. Marge asked, pulling her aside. "What's wrong?"

"I'm just tired. I was up late studying. I still have the binder markings on my face from my notebook where I fell asleep working on a paper," she dramatically pointed to a cheek.

"Well, I'm afraid that you are going to have to focus. You have already switched up the orders for at least two tables."

"I'll try harder," Nadine promised, wondering how many cups of coffee Ms. Marge would let her consume before it started coming out of her paycheck.

"You'll do better regardless of how hard you try," her boss demanded before going back to the register. She felt bad for Allen's daughter, but as a business owner, she could not allow her servers to be sloppy in either appearance or service.

"Yes ma'am," fell on deaf ears as the late breakfast crowd became the early lunch crowd without a moment's rest to get some homework done.

Chapter 4

Fairy Tales

"Nadine!" Heather called from her bedroom. "I'm ready for breakfast!"

Rolling her eyes, Nadine mumbled, "Then come downstairs and eat at the table like the rest of us are forced to do."

"What was that?" Heather's excellent hearing called back.

"I'll be there in five minutes," Nadine called back. "Sooner if you didn't insist on bacon and eggs every morning," she finished, mumbling again.

"Three minutes!"

"I'll try."

"You'll do better than try!"

Rolling her eyes, again, Nadine would suspect that Heather had planted listening devices around the house if it wasn't for the fact that Nadine was the only person who apparently knew how to clean the house. If there were any listening devices around then she would have found it. Even still, she eyed the pesky kitchen intercom with a look of distrust.

Four minutes later, she was walking up the stairs carrying a breakfast tray after pulling the pre-cooked bacon - a necessary grocery splurge - out of the microwave and tossing the pan she used to fry the eggs in the sink to soak.

While she knew that the pan would be soaking in that sink until she got home after her evening shift at the diner, it was better to let it soak instead of letting the leftover egg stick to the pan.

"Two fried eggs and three pieces of bacon," Nadine held out to Heather before slowly backing out of the room. She had twenty minutes before she was due in her first class for the day.

Sliding into her seat for her Survey of World Literature class, Nadine looked around. Eight in the morning was far too early for a class, but it fit into her busy schedule perfectly. Class at eight, the diner at ten, repeat throughout the week. Monday, Wednesday, and Fridays were her hour-long literature class and Tuesday and Thursdays were her hour and a half long history class. Somehow, she had managed to grab a spot in one of the online math classes.

The combined assigned reading lists were staggering. The necessary papers for both classes were time-consuming. Coffee had become her best friend.

"Oral traditions were one of the earliest forms of storytelling. Can anybody tell me why?"

Raising her hand, Nadine answered, "People were poor. Most of them could not read or write, let alone afford a leather-bound, handwritten book."

"Correct," the professor smiled. "That's also why you can find so many different versions of some tales. That's why a good portion of these tales rhyme or have descriptors that help the audience recall who is being talked about. Examples?"

"Greek Myth!" somebody called out.

"Beowulf."

"Fairy tales," Nadine blurted out without thinking. Her face warmed as everybody turned to look at her. A few of the girls even giggled while a few guys rolled their eyes.

Grinning even more, the professor looked at the class. "And on that note," she grabbed a handful of printed of pages, "we have our introduction. Does anybody know how many versions of Sleeping Beauty there are?"

"At least five," Nadine answered. "Basile, Perrault, and Brothers Grimm - but I've seen at least two or three variations of their version - and Calvino. Joseph Jacobs also included a version in his *More English Fairy Tales* collection."

The professor, stunned for a moment, looked down at her notes. The Freshman's answer was much more thorough than she expected.

"That also doesn't include the various movie and cartoon versions," Nadine concluded.

"Cinderella?"

"Eight: Basile, Perrault, and Brothers Grimm along with an Ancient Greek, older British, China, West Asia, and Vietnam all have versions."

"Snow White?"

"Six from other countries and multiple variations from the Brothers Grimm themselves including changing it from a jealous mother to a jealous step-mother."

"Beauty and the Beast?"

Nadine took a deep breath before answering, "At least four that I'm aware of."

"Four?"

"The original written by Gabrielle-Suzanne Barbot de Villeneuve, the abridged versions by Jeanne-Marie Leprince de Beaumont and Andrew Lang, as well as a version from the Brothers Grimm titled Lily and the Lion that seems to be a combination of *Beauty and the Beast* and *East of the Sun and West of the Moon*."

All the professor could do was nod her head and smile, "Excellent. Somebody knows her fairy tales." Her own research didn't uncover the last variation. "Today you'll get into pairs or groups of three, pick a tale, and tell me about the variations you have seen or read - yes, book and movie. You'll write down how they differ, how they are similar, and how these variations might have been influenced by the time periods they were written in. Do not write on my packets and turn everything in by the end of class. Your assignment for the weekend is on the board."

Nadine watched as her professor collapsed in her seat. She didn't mean to show off like she had, but it had happened and now her classmates were nearly fighting over who was going to be paired up with her. It was a huge change from a few minutes ago when they thought she was being childish for even mentioning fairy tales.

Pointing at two classmates she suspected would do their share of the work, she stood up before stating, "Alyson and Jessica." Pausing, "I'll be right back; I'll go get our packet."

Heading over to the professor, Nadine tried to smile. "I'm sorry," Nadine stated, reaching for one of the packets.

"How did you know all of that?" her teacher sighed. "Nobody ever does."

Looking at the table, Nadine whispered, "My mother collected fairy tales. She insisted on reading them to me before she died, or so my father told me. When I was eight I discovered her collection. That was about the time my father remarried so I used the books as a way to connect to my mother. They were some of the few books I've ever kept over the years and I still go back to them on occasion."

"I understand." And the crazy part was, Nadine thought her professor really did understand how Nadine had used the tales to keep part of her mother's memory alive.

Feet aching, Nadine counted down the minutes until her shift ended. In the back of her mind, she was still replaying the odd lesson in class. She never expected a professor to bring in fairy tales about a lesson on oral tradition.

All that lesson did was remind Nadine of all of the fairy tales her mother had read to her before Lindsey Harrington Witt's car accident when Nadine was six. It reminded her of the book she had hidden underneath her bed.

"Nadine!" Ms. Marge called from the cash register. "Order up!" she pointed towards the window.

Holding back a deep sigh, she shook her head, walked over to the pass-through window, and collected her plates. She only had to take it to this one table and she could go home and dig into her math class assignment.

But, thanks to class, her mind wasn't on math or her last table. It was on a distant memory of a boy named Richmond and his rose garden. It had been a long time since she had last thought of that boy in the woods.

Sometimes, however, she would get this feeling as if she was being watched, but a quick look around her told her that it must have been part of her overactive imagination. Sure, there were times where her instincts were correct, but it usually happened when some part of her plans were about to fall apart spectacularly.

"Nadine!" Ms. Marge called back, the phone cradled against her ear. "Meg can't come in. I need you to cover her shift."

Closing her eyes, Nadine tiredly resisted the urge to cry. "I've already been working for six hours. I'm supposed to get off as soon as my last table leaves," she whispered once she had gotten closer to where Ms. Marge was standing.

"Then you'll just take a break and clock back in after an hour," Ms. Marge shrugged. "It's only for four hours. You don't even have to close," she finished matter-a-fact.

Shortly after ten o'clock, Nadine found herself crawling on her knees in front of her bed. Glancing back to make certain that her bedroom door was still shut, she pulled out the one fairy tale book that had not come from her mother. Even these tales were slightly different than the ones displayed on her bookcase and that worried her. Instead, they were hidden carefully inside the box spring of her mattress.

"Nadine!" she heard as footsteps pounded up the stairs leading to her attic bedroom. "Nadine!" her stepmother's voice echoed. "I'm ready for dinner!"

"Coming," Nadine called back, wondering why her stepmother couldn't have made herself something at a more reasonable hour instead of waiting for Nadine to come home from work. It wasn't as if she hadn't called to let Heather know that she was picking up Meg's shift.

Wrapping the book back up in an old shirt, she pushed it under the bed and towards the wall instead of back into its hiding place. Maybe she would have time to read it after her stepmother had gone back to bed.

That never happened and Nadine forgot to hide the book back in its secure location. Instead, she remembered the math assignment that she was supposed to be completing and found herself with yet another late night seated at her desk.

Chapter 5

Enter Charming

- About One Year Before -

It had easily taken a year for Angela to find just the right place to work. Not everybody was as easily manipulated as Ms. Marge, wanting proof of identity papers and the like. When you have traveled through unsanctioned portals from the Enchanted Forest into "The Real World" there were no papers to help smooth over matters.

Instead, Angela had to use her magic to subtly manipulate Ms. Marge into hiring her, when she hadn't been hiring at the moment, and to convince her fellow co-workers that her taking some of their hours was not an issue.

It took another three weeks to get Nadine to drop her guard down long enough to trust Angela, for them to become best friends. Angela would find herself helping Nadine out far too often, accepting shifts she didn't want to take in order to ensure that Nadine could have some time to herself.

They never went out and did anything; Nadine had far too much on her plate for that with her job, stepmother, and stepsister.

Best of all, whenever she could, Angela would send a tiny bit of magic - not enough to send out a signal flare to alert other magic users of her presence - in Meg's direction to trip her up.

Sometimes plates of food went flying through the air, never landing on customers but occasionally landing in Meg's hair. Once a plate landed on Ms. Marge; for some reason, their boss had been particularly harsh with Nadine that day.

That was the one thing Angela never could figure out; why was Ms. Marge harder towards Nadine than anybody else? She knew that Heather Witt had sold Ms. Marge what was then the bakery even though she had no legal claim to it excepting that Nadine was a week away from turning eighteen and Heather still had legal rights over her stepdaughter despite Allen Witt's will.

Angela knew that Nadine had no way of reclaiming her inheritance. Heather had spent every last dime of it on the mortgage and who knew what else. But she couldn't help but wonder, did Ms. Marge think keeping Nadine under her thumb would prevent the now nearly twenty-year-old from claiming something she could no longer get back?

Angela looked at her friend as the girls busily removed the dishes from the table. Nadine had enough walls built around her to form a tower. The lack of time to get a haircut had her light brown hair, even when in a ponytail, over halfway down her back. At any moment she expected somebody to burst into the restaurant and cry, "Rapunzel, Rapunzel let down your hair!"

The scene was so vivid in her mind that she fully expected it to happen.

That was when a rose-colored haze filled her vision and things began to sparkle, but she still saw the scene, clear as day. Nadine was busy scrubbing down a table as a bewildered college student entered the diner, his blonde hair creating a halo effect as the sun hit the strands. Looking up, his face relaxed at the sight of Nadine. Then...

"Ange?" Nadine poked her, a concerned look on her face. "Where are you?"

Confused, "I'm right here?" the other server answered.

"No, seriously; you spaced out for a moment."

"That's the thing, I was right here. I saw..." but before she could describe her vision, a group of ten entered the diner. "I'll tell you later." She smiled before greeting the customers. She never got to tell Nadine what she had envisioned.

"What do you mean you can't find my daughter?" the Queen slowly asked her nephew.

Hesitating, Sawyer straightened up and took a deep breath. "I went looking for your cousin, Lindsey Harrington Witt, but all I found…" he handed over a newspaper article and a photo. "I'm sorry."

Taking a quick look at the items he handed over, Gabrielle scanned for the relevant details including the information about Allen Witt and her daughter, Nadine. "What happened to Allen Witt?"

Handing over another article Sawyer said nothing. Just waited.

"Two car accidents. That's odd," she mumbled to herself. Turning towards her Spade, she instructed, "Check the fairy tales and Traditions."

Stephan looked at his son before asking, "Is there a stepmother in the picture?"

"Ummm…" Sawyer mumbled, flipping through the pieces of paper in his hands. "I…"

"Go find out," his father snapped, disappointed and surprised that his normally steadfast third son hadn't already thought about seeing if there was a stepmother involved; that would significantly reduce the number of fairy tales pulling Nadine in their direction.

"Yes, sir," he jerked to attention before scattering.

They waited until Sawyer had disappeared until Gabrielle turned to look at him. "Can he do this?"

"Yes," the Spade answered passionately, certain that his son was capable of locating the missing princess.

Leaning backward on the throne, she studied him. "What fairy tale is she currently in?"

"If there is a stepmother involved Nadine is in Cinderella. Maybe Snow White if there are no stepsiblings."

"And if there is no stepmother?"

Stephan scanned his brain, trying to think of a tale about an orphaned daughter. There were plenty of tales with stepmothers, but none came to mind without a stepmother. "I don't know."

Standing up, she started to pace the floor before asking him, "What happened to the Hall of Tales? I see it everywhere in my family journals, but I don't know where it is."

"It disappears every so often for about a hundred years," he confusedly answered her. "Where did that information come from?"

They looked at each other before stating, "The Forgotten Story."

Slowly, the Queen whispered, "Only we don't know what that story is anymore."

"But," the Spade smiled, "we will soon." There was only one Traditional reason why princesses would go missing and that wasn't kidnapping - Nadine was on a Quest.

Straightening up, Angela scanned the diner as a feeling of déjà vu passed through her. Nadine was leaning over a table collecting plates and generally bussing a table while their usual busboy was on his break. The sun was sparkling through the just washed windows - Mrs. Marge insisted that they were professionally washed every week.

Opening the outside door, a tall, golden-haired university student entered the bakery. "I thought this was a bakery," he mumbled to his friend as they looked around them.

"This is a bakery," Nadine answered him from the other side of the door where she was juggling a stack of plates and glasses. "Ms. Marge added some lunch and dinner menu items using our baked goods." Despite the years that Ms. Marge insisted on calling the place a diner, Nadine knew in her heart that this place was truly a bakery with meal items.

"Like?" the friend asked, nudging the blonde back to attention.

"Deli club sandwiches. Chicken potpie made with freshly made dough. On occasion, the kitchen makes chicken and dumplings. Other sandwiches, pies, breads, and the like. There's a menu on the table if you are interested in taking a look."

"Oh, I'm interested," the blonde smiled while his friend shook his head in disbelief. "I'm Guy Westmore," he introduced himself.

"Nadine Witt," she smiled back.

"A pleasure."

His friend rolled his eyes. He couldn't recall how many times Guy applied his charm to get what he wanted. Blinking, he realized that no clear examples came to mind, but he knew it happened, even if he couldn't remember it happening in detail.

"Is there a phone we can use?" Guy whispered, leaning in towards Nadine. "My car ran out of gas just outside this place and this guy's cell phone battery died." He used to thumb to point towards his friend.

The friend added, "And he didn't even bring his phone."

Resisting the urge to roll her own eyes, Nadine nodded her head towards the counter. "There's a phone by the cash register, however, it's for paying customers only. Bakery rules." She sent him an uncharacteristic wink as she disappeared behind the doors leading towards the dishwasher.

Without a word, the unnamed friend turned towards where Angela had been watching the scene. "Which section is your friend's so that Guy here can continue making a fool out of himself?"

"Over there," Angela reluctantly pointed. She had a bad feeling about all of this but was powerless to stop it. Literally. She had used all that she was willing to spare in causing Meg to drop a plate covered in waffle pieces and syrup on her legs.

Guy, noticing Angela for the first time, froze for a moment. A pins and needles sensation invaded his conscience, but he quickly pushed it away and dismissed it. Blinking, he looked away before sauntering over to an empty table in Nadine's section.

If Guy didn't recognize her then Angela wasn't going to remind him.

Shaking his head, Guy's friend urged him to hurry up. He had a feeling that he was supposed to be somewhere else even if he couldn't recall where he was supposed to be at.

"Don't be so impatient," Guy snapped. "I'm paying for your meal."

Shaking his head, "Don't you ever feel like you are supposed to be doing something?"

"All the time," Guy snapped, handing over a menu. "Now, pick something that looks good."

Within a few minutes, Nadine joined them at their table, her notepad out and ready to take their orders. "What can I get you to drink?"

"I'll have a Coke," Guy grinned, "And Charles here will have a sweet tea."

Charles only blinked; a dazed and confused look on his face as if he was trying to remember something.

"Okay," Nadine smiled at both of them. "I'll be back in a minute with your drinks."

"Take your time," Guy smirked. "We aren't in a rush."

Richmond paced the empty hallways, hearing the echoing of his boots against the marble flooring. If there was anybody around, and there had to be somebody around since the mundane everyday things like meals kept getting done, then they weren't visible.

Instead, he only had the echo of his boots and the rebounding of his voice bouncing around in the castle. It was enough to slowly drive him insane after over a hundred years.

"It wasn't supposed to take this long!" he roared! "One hundred years! Not three!" The words bounced back at him.

He didn't want to think about the impact this was making on the Enchanted Forest.

Twelve years ago, shortly after the little princess Nadine had found her way into the rose garden and discovered the magic rose, he had begun to grow older. When he was sixteen and started feeling the horns starting to sprout out of his head, Richmond covered the mirrors. At twenty it was the hair. Twenty-one his fangs began growing in. Very recently, at twenty-four, his final change began to happen and his hands turned into claws.

As he had neared twenty-four, he started wondering why he was only half-human and half-beast. Why he was still able to wear boots and still fit into most of his clothes.

On occasion he'd rip a shirt while working out; he refused to work out without a shirt on because at least then he could pretend that his body wasn't mostly covered in coarse fur-like hair.

"Where are you, Nadine?" he grumbled while continuing to pace back and forth.

Chapter 6

Odds and Ends

Letting out a sigh as Guy walked into the room, Angela leaned over the table she was wiping down with Nadine and whispered, "I think there's more to Guy than he's letting on."

"What do you mean?" Nadine whispered back, watching over her shoulder as Guy made his way into her section and settled into a booth.

Today he was alone. It happened more and more often. Some days he would have a friend with him; a friend, Angela had noted on more than one occasion, that seemed as if he was not completely certain where he was or who he was. And they all noticed that he was coming in alone more and more often.

Grabbing Nadine's arm, Angela kept her friend in place. "He shows up every Friday at the same time..."

"...He just got out of class..." Nadine interrupted.

The other server continued as if her friend had not interrupted her, "And sits in the exact same four-seater booth..."

Shrugging a shoulder, Nadine dismissed her co-worker's implication that he was taking up valuable restaurant seating real estate. "He normally has friends with him…"

"And takes up most of your time, causing you to neglect your other customers and tippers." Okay, maybe Angela had a point there.

It took a long pause before Nadine mumbled, "He more than makes up for it."

Angela started shaking her head, "No, Nadine," she sighed. "He's making you dependent on him." Even she knew that the hundred dollar tips wouldn't last forever, especially if Ms. Marge decided to fire Nadine for poor service. Angela had a feeling that Ms. Marge was looking for a reason to get rid of Nadine for some reason she had yet to detect.

With a roll of her eyes, Nadine muttered, "Whatever," and made her way to where he was sitting. "Afternoon, Guy. Are you getting your usual?"

But she was still worried. She'd heard rumors from the other servers that he also showed up again after Nadine's shift was over on Fridays or during the Saturday afternoon shift between two and six - during Nadine's four-hour break during her longest day.

She had no clue how Nadine would react if she shared her suspicions that Guy was also talking to Meg.

"I can't go out with you," Nadine sighed as she slipped around the tables in the dining room and collected the salt and pepper shakers at the empty tables. Guy never had stuck around so long before, and she needed to get her work done before she could leave.

Tonight was the night to wash the glass shakers and if she didn't get the salt and pepper poured into their storage containers - in this instance clean and dry tea pitchers that would be covered with plastic wrap and aluminum foil - then the busboys would be delayed as well since they had to wash them.

If the busboys finished quickly enough, and the shakers dried, Angela and Nadine would get to refill the shakers and set them back out before they even left for the night. It would save them from having to do that task in the morning.

"Why not?" a persistent Guy asked, taking the tray that carried the shakers from her hands.

Moving towards the next table, Nadine answered honestly as she sat the shakers on the tray. "My step-mother would kill me if I went out with anybody."

"You are twenty years old. She can't stop you from dating anybody."

"Not while I'm living under her roof," she scoffed. He missed her eye roll.

"Then move out," Guy suggested.

"Right," she sarcastically agreed. "That's easier said than done," she added in case he didn't catch onto her sarcasm.

Sometimes, Nadine had noticed, tones and expressions went over Guy's head. It was almost as if he wasn't from around here. It wasn't something she focused on; many of the student customers that came in here weren't always from the area. That was part of the benefits of having so many colleges and the community college nearby.

"Why is that?"

How could she explain that she didn't want to lose her childhood home? She doubted that he would even understand what her home meant to her, even if she claimed the attic as her personal space. Even she knew that someday Heather would get tired of their financial state and find husband number three. Since Nadine's name was also on the house deed, Heather simply couldn't sell it out from underneath her.

"I can't explain it," she weakly answered him after thinking about it for a long moment.

"That tells me nothing," Guy grumbled, grunting a bit when he lifted the shaker tray.

Taking it out of his hands, Nadine walked over to the server prep station and started unscrewing saltshaker tops.

Joining her on the other side of the counter, he steadfastly ignored Angela.

Nadine could feel her friend tensing up next to her. Out of the corner of her eye, she thought she saw a glittery sheen covering Angela. Turning to look at her fully, her co-worker looked the same, no shimmer surrounding her after all.

"What?" Angela asked, catching Nadine's odd look.

Shaking her head, she dismissed what she thought she saw as mere exhaustion. "Nothing. It was nothing," she whispered with a headshake. Turning to address Guy, she added, "I need to get some work done. I'll see you in a few days."

Nodding his head, Guy turned around and walked out the door.

Rolling her eyes, Angela spoke up for the first time since Guy had entered the diner that evening. "I don't like him."

"You have told me that before," Nadine sighed, pouring the salt from the shakers into the pitcher in front of her.

It was draining having to eat the same thing over and over again during the week. Tuesday evenings - Chicken potpie during Meg's shift. Wednesday evenings - Deli Club sandwich during Nadine's shift. Friday lunch - Another Deli Club. Saturday afternoon - Another chicken pot pie.

So far nobody was talking to the girls and telling them that he was playing them both. However, conversations with Meg led him to believe that she would have no problem knowing that he was seeing her behind Nadine's back.

"They are going to find out," his reluctant roommate chided him.

"As long as I've accomplished my mission before they do."

He felt his humanity slipping as the curse began to fully take effect. This told him that she would be returning soon. Hopefully sooner rather than later; the longer he remained without any human contact the more beast-like he became.

His roars no longer startled the sparrows and wrens that had taken up residence in the upper rafters of the halls. A pair of doves had built a nest in a corner of the dining hall. Red birds. Blue jays. Bluebirds.

All sorts of birds that had once been frightened by his roar barely ruffled a feather when they heard his growl echoing down the castle. They knew he wouldn't harm them unlike the deer and animals of prey that he did chase down for a meal when the kitchen's offerings weren't enough.

The final sign was when the metal rose in the garden began to bloom.

He had one year.

Chapter 7

Unexpected

Dragging her tired self into the kitchen, Nadine looked up towards the ceiling as the annoyingly loud music seeped through the floors. Releasing a sigh she felt deep in her bones, she shook her head before moving to dig into the fridge. "I'm too tired for this," she whimpered as she pulled out things for Heather's meal and a sandwich for herself.

Once her sandwich was finished and Nadine started putting everything up. Turning around, she watched as Heather entered the room and grabbed her dinner, along with Nadine's sandwich, without a single comment except, "Tell Meg and her guest to turn down their music. It's giving me a headache."

"Yes, Ma'am," Nadine sighed, regathering her sandwich supplies to make herself another sandwich. She wasn't surprised when Heather said nothing about Nadine's birthday.

Finally, five minutes later, sandwich in hand, she pulled herself up the stairs and made her way to Meg's door.

"Meg!" she loudly knocked. "Open up!"

She was extremely tempted to admonish Meg for missing her afternoon shift at the bakery causing Nadine to work well over twelve hours. Nadine was tired, exhausted truthfully, and things she had kept bottled up for years were threatening to spill over.

Once the door opened, she barged in and started talking. "Where were you tonight? Marge had me work your shift in addition to…" Nadine stopped her furious ranting once the full force of the scene in front of her finally caught up with her brain. "Guy."

Meg had opened the door wrapped in one of her sheets, the smirk on her face growing as Nadine's face began to fall. Guy chuckling from his place on the bed as he finished pulling on his boxers.

"Did you really think he was actually interested in you?" Meg smirked, excited that she was able to take something away from the almost perfect Nadine.

Escaping her stepsister's room, Nadine dashed up the attic stairs to her room.

"Nadine!" Guy called out behind her, tugging on his jeans as he stumbled his way out of Meg's room. "Wait!"

"Go away!" she shouted back at him.

"Nadine! Come on!"

"Go away!" she turned and threw the nearest object she could reach at him.

Guy's concerned face, plastered on his face once Nadine had darted out of Meg's room, transformed into a grin as he stepped foot into the room. "I've been looking for you for a really long time…" he drawled, moving his fingers over Nadine's things as he started circling her room. "Ever since you were eight and left the Enchanted Forest with a certain book in hand."

With a flick of his hand, he had frozen her in place. Despite trying to move, Nadine couldn't figure out why she couldn't move an inch, except for her eyes. He wanted her watching him.

Watching his progress around the room, she resisted the urge to glance towards the space under the bed. "I don't know what you are talking about."

Circling her, Guy rolled his eyes. "Thirteen years ago you accidentally entered the Enchanted Forest and the Forgotten Kingdom. You met a boy a little older than you were and found a magic rose that was neither metal nor plant. He... Wasn't his name Richmond?" Guy paused in his recitation to ask. When Nadine said nothing, he continued telling his story. "Richmond handed over this old-fashioned looking book of fairy tales. Leather bound, gold leaf edges, and lettering. Ring a bell?"

Turning to look at her bookcase, he scanned the titles that remained on her shelves. When nothing looked familiar, he turned back towards her. "This book is special. Magical." His face turning into stone, Guy's eyes narrowed. "Where is the book?"

Eyes steadily meeting his, Nadine calmly stated, "That's an interesting story." Years of lying to the steps helped her maintain eye contact. "Too bad I don't know what you're talking about."

Nodding his head in acknowledgment, he grinned, "You make a very good liar." He released the holding spell with a flick of his fingers.

Shrugging a shoulder and taking a bite out of her sandwich, she made him wait before saying, "I still don't know what you are talking about." Part of her enjoyed the veins that were starting to appear on his temples. Another part of her was scared of him even if she refused to show it.

"Yes, you do," he hissed, stalking inches away from her face before backing away towards the bookcases.

"Who are you?" she quietly asked him, suddenly terrified of the expression she had seen in his eyes.

Once again prowling around the room while keeping an eye on her, "Somebody who has been waiting a really long time for Richmond's curse to be almost lifted," he snapped. Nadine felt as if he was stalking his prey - her.

"Why?" she calmly asked, taking another bite of sandwich. The bread seemed dry and everything gummed up in her mouth as she chewed. Nadine prayed frantically that he couldn't sense how fast her heart was pumping.

Leaning forward - but not as close as before - Guy whispered, "He's not the only one cursed."

"Why me?"

When she started to move Guy froze her in place with a flick of his wrist. "Because you are the catalyst that sets everything into motion and without you I'm stuck here." Shaking his head, he continued to scan the room looking for the book. "Do you think it was easy manipulating you and Meg? Timing is not something that magic can control. It helped that Meg already disliked you, wanting everything you have. It wasn't difficult to show up during her shifts either, also looking like Prince Charming in trouble. A little hand gesture," he demonstrated, "and I could create brilliant rays of sunlight backlighting me."

Meg, standing in the doorway, gave a little gasp. "You used me?"

Cutting his eyes in her direction, "Of course I did. I need that fairy tale book."

Meg purred from the doorway, unconcerned about everything she had overheard while eavesdropping in the hallway. "You mean the one that Nadine keeps under her bed?"

Knowing it was pointless, Nadine hissed, "Meg!"

"Thank, my dear," Guy grinned at her. "You have been a big help."

Before Meg could move, he froze her in place as well. He didn't need her stopping him from getting the book, even though she wouldn't. What he really didn't need was her being clingy and trying to convince him to take her with him.

Thankfully Meg would forget all about him soon enough.

Reaching underneath the bed, he pulled out the book and grinned at the girls. Snipping any begging and pleading in the bud, he smirked before stating, "Meg, my dear, I would bring you back to the Enchanted Forest with me, however, I doubt Mother would be very thrilled with having a whiny mortal screwing up her peace and quiet." Turning to Nadine, "I'm sure I will see you again before Richmond's curse is broken." Within moments, and without a portal, Guy disappeared.

All he needed was the magic from the book to be able to transport himself where he needed to be next. There he could lay in wait for his next move.

With his disappearance, both girls collapsed on the floor. It took Meg a while before she could ask, "What just happened?"

"You just told the villain where to find the key to destroy all the fairy tales in the world." Nadine paused before adding, "Or possibly just one of them…"

Without another thought towards her steps or the books still collecting dust on her bookcases, she reached into her closet and pulled out the first sweatshirt she could grab - a red-hooded sweatshirt at that - and grabbed her purse where she had dropped it when she'd rushed into her room. The garage had everything else she needed.

Heather and Meg could figure out how to take care of themselves. None of this would have happened if Meg didn't want to claim everything Nadine had, including boyfriends.

It barely mattered that Guy had found Nadine first; those thoughts would haunt her later. Right now she had to find a way to get back to Richmond.

Chapter 8

Return to the Cursed Garden

The race to Richmond's estate was not as uneventful as she had expected it to be. Nadine had assumed that once Guy had disappeared with the book that it would be the last time she saw him.

She didn't know that he needed to know where her portal was.

It had been thirteen years since she had last visited the campground that had started it all. She could remember the general location of where she had always gone camping with her father, but locating the path to Richmond's gardens would be the problem.

Pulling into the parking lot, Nadine looked at her car. It had taken a good amount of persuasion and logic to convince Heather to let her use Matt's old car instead of selling it when he left it behind, and even then she had to share it with Meg. She suspected that Heather had only agreed so that Nadine could get to work and go get groceries.

Staring at the keys in her hands, the only thing she knew was that she did not plan on returning.

Unlocking the doors, she nearly tossed the keys inside behind her before pausing. Digging into her backpack, she pulled out a notebook and scribbled down a note on where to return the car and that she was never returning to that house. Nadine didn't have a clue that as soon as she stepped through the portal that the car would return to Heather's driveway - without the note - and that everything concerning her would be removed from Heather, Meg, Matt, and Mrs. Marge's memories.

Only Angela could remember her.

Tossing the note and keys into the driver's side seat, she slammed the door shut, shifted her backpack filled with a notebook, a few water bottles, and snacks. She would have added a camping hammock to the mix, only she had no intention of stopping and sleeping.

It was already late and Nadine was aware that she was risking injury by hiking into the woods after nightfall, but she didn't have much of a choice. She wasn't staying under Heather's roof one more night and she didn't have a clue where Angela lived.

Halfway to the campsites, she felt a prickle on her neck as if she was being watched. Turning around, she scanned the area for fellow hikers also getting a late start but saw nothing. Shaking her head, she carried on while attempting to ignore the feeling of being observed.

After thirty minutes of hiking, she finally managed to locate the campsites, all of which were empty in November. Closing her eyes, she tried to focus on her memory of the last trip. Nodding her head, Nadine turned and started walking towards the trail that led towards the lake. It twisted and turned, but she could recall that she had taken that trail.

She wasn't aware that something else was pulling her towards where she needed to go. She could have closed her eyes and the Tradition would have guided her to Richmond's gates.

"Okay, Nadine," she whispered aloud to herself. "That fallen tree trunk might not be there anymore."

Even her whisper seemed to echo throughout the trees.

"Oh," Guy purred behind her from where he was leaning against a tree, "that fallen tree trunk was removed several years ago. You'll have to rely on instinct."

Freezing in place, Nadine took a moment to take a deep breath and hide her panic. Finally, she hissed, "What are you doing here?"

"Do you really think I'm going to just let you return to Richmond?"

"You already have the book," she pointed out. "What more do you need?"

Cackling from behind her caught her attention. "Well," a female old enough to be Guy's mother and dressed as the stereotypical evil fairy smirked, "preventing you from reaching the Enchanted Forest would be ideal."

"The Enchanted Forest?"

Laughing, Guy redirected Nadine's attention. "Oh, my dear, you have a lot to learn."

Looking back and forth between them, she closed her eyes for a moment. Taking a deep breath, she couldn't let them know that she'd noticed something behind a fallen tree trunk that shimmered.

Reaching behind her, she took off her backpack before unzipping it and pulling out a water bottle.

"What are you doing?" the evil-looking fairy hissed.

"I need something to drink," Nadine answered her, holding up her bottle of water. Holding up a bag, she asked, "Does anybody want any trail mix?"

Shaking his head, Guy missed his mother tilting her head in curiosity. "What is trail mix?"

"This is," Nadine threw the contents of the bag in the fairy's face before turning and squeezing her water bottle in Guy's face. Without a second thought, she darted towards the fallen tree and the portal that was behind it.

"Get her!" the fairy called out. "She can't enter that portal!"

Right as she entered the shimmery thing - a portal if she heard the fairy right - she could feel Guy tugging on her shirt. Thankfully, her momentum was enough to propel them both forward, cutting off the fairy's shrieking.

Landing at an unexpected roll, Nadine lost valuable time trying to get back on her feet. Guy managed to pull on her hair or shirt in order to pull her back down.

Finally, after struggling for several minutes, she managed to land a kick to his knee. It felt really good to land a blow after catching him cheating on her with Meg. Darting off, she couldn't help but wonder why he didn't just freeze her in place as he had done in her room.

After a few more minutes, the rusted gate appeared. It opened as she approached it before slamming shut in Guy's face. Leaning forward, Nadine gasped for breath as Guy shook the gates.

Ignoring the various names he called her, she started to stumble forward towards the house. It was easy to catch the differences that thirteen years had caused.

The woods were dense around the house that no longer gave the appearance of being a mere house. She had sworn that she would never return. That what had happened when she was a child had been a daydream.

It had been a fruitless promise to herself. *He* was the only person who could help her. *He* was the only person who knew what to do. *He* was the only person who had haunted her dreams for the past thirteen years.

"Let me in!" she shouted, pounding on the doors and praying that he was home. "I need your help!" Everything around her was dark, *but it is late*, she reasoned. *Almost midnight,* her panicked mind helpfully stated. He would have to allow the crazy girl banging on the windows in the house, wouldn't he? "Please," she began to sob, looking behind her at the gate she had entered, hoping that Guy could not get past the fence. "I need you."

From the shadows of the garden, he had watched her frantic run down the drive, through the rose garden gate, and up to the entryway of his house. Its glamour had begun to fade away that morning and soon the façade of a normal house would completely return to its original castle form. He did not move until her sobbing had left her leaning against the door, immobile.

She did not see him approach, barely felt him picking her up and taking her inside. His heat warmed her chilled body and the tears kept pouring out of her as her tense muscles relaxed slightly from his warmth and the fact that she now knew that he would help her. "I'm sorry. I know I promised to never come back."

"It is okay," he mumbled, managing to lock the door behind them. He knew that she had no choice in the matter. "Tell me what happened."

"Guy found the book," she whispered before passing out from exhaustion and relief. It had been a long day between work and running away, not to forget the emotional turmoil she had experienced in learning about Guy's true nature.

A few hours later, finding herself curled up on a bed, Nadine jerked upright and frantically looked around the room before the memory of her race to find Richmond and tell him about the theft of the book she had been guarding since she was eight and had stumbled on the twelve-year-old boy.

"It is okay," Richmond comforted her from where he had resumed hiding in the shadows. "The book was meant to be stolen."

"You could have told me *that* thirteen years ago!" she mumbled, looking for her red hoodie. "Where is my red hoodie?"

"It is put away." Still standing in the shadows, "Do you know the significance of that book?"

"It was just a book of fairy tales." She started to stand up but found herself still too tired to move. She wondered if Guy had found where she had left her car at the head of the trail leading to the house in the woods. She had no clue that it had been returned to Heather's driveway the moment she stumbled through the portal.

Only it wasn't really a house anymore, was it?

"And do you know which tale you are currently in?"

Nadine sat up, her eyes wide. "That was real?" She blinked. "But I kissed that frog and nothing happened."

Richmond laughed, the rumble sending pleasant shivers down her spine, "You never finished reading that tale. In the original story, the frog was thrown against the wall." Leaning against the wall, the shadows hiding him even further, "And a few other tales have gone unfinished because you never read the book aloud completely."

Pausing, he added, "In some instances that is a good thing."

Nadine's eyes widened. "It all started that day I was lost in the woods and found you."

"Hansel and Gretel, minus Hansel," he supplied.

She added, "The Frog Prince."

"Cinderella," Richmond retorted.

Slowly she whispered, "Little Red Riding Hood." Nadine's head jerked at that tale, thinking of the red hoodie she favored. "Are you the wolf then?"

Drawing a deep breath, Richmond relied on knowledge he knew by magical means. "No. Guy was until you escaped him."

Closing her eyes as if she dreaded the answer, "Then what tale am I currently living in?"

"Beauty and the Beast." Stepping out of the shadows, he let her see his bearded face. It was a drastic change from the young boy he once was and the man he was today. The new addition, the part that let him know that Nadine was soon to arrive, were the claws where his hands should have been. "This will be your last tale since Guy stole the book from you."

Holding back her shriek of surprise, Nadine felt the mantle of Tradition falling over her. Now she believed that the tales in that book, and probably others, were real.

That didn't mean she had to like it.

The Queen of Wonderland let out a sigh of relief when the Spade's son, now also a Spade, approached her. "Nadine is in the Enchanted Forest, My Lady," he bowed.

Laughing with relief, she teased her nephew, "Sawyer, you are my nephew; there is no reason to 'My Lady' me to death."

"Yes, Aunt."

"Now, where is my daughter?"

"She's in the Forgotten Kingdom."

"The Forgotten Kingdom? Which tale is that?" She looked over at the Record's Keeper she had been discussing Alice's best matches with when Sawyer the Spade had entered the room.

He froze for a moment before answering. "We won't know until the curse is broken. Nobody knows, not even the records themselves."

"How is that possible?"

This time he shrugged his shoulders before answering, "Magic."

"Of course. Do let me know when these records reappear and about that matter we were just discussing." Turning back to Sawyer, she said, "Go tell your father and uncles. I'll tell my husband."

Part Two

Chapter 9

Exploring

Nadine's arrival signaled a change in the way things had to be done.

The servants, uncertain how she was going to react to invisible people going around doing the essential everyday tasks, remained silent and became even more careful than before her arrival. A few of them had realized that they would be able to converse with Nadine and Richmond now when the two 'humans' had turned their heads in the direction of the chatting servants down the hall.

They hadn't been able to talk to Richmond before, even if he had talked to them in an attempt to hold onto part of his humanity. None of them, excepting Cook and the butler, could read or write; not that the Cook and the butler were very receptive towards 'talking' to the master of the estate. After a week of attempting to get various servants to write down on the slates he found in the abandoned schoolroom, Richmond ended up throwing the slates in a fit of frustration, breaking them into unusable pieces.

Even though he was aware that he would now have somebody to talk to, he tended to focus on other things. Thinking about his new companion meant that he would have to face the knowledge that he had no clue how to talk to other people anymore. He had spent most of his time talking to people who could not talk back or reading most of the books in his library - until he was unable to read anymore thanks to his claws.

No, there was one more thing that he was excited about.

One good thing about all of this, Richmond thought, *was that the scouts would be returning soon.* They would probably be the third or fourth generation of the scouts his father had sent out, and hopefully, they would have been informed of their roles as the older generations passed on, but they would be bringing advancements in technology when they finally arrived.

With any luck, a new Cook would be among those masses. He wasn't thrilled with the way his current cook treated the people around him.

Soon the castle could be bustling with people and he would no longer be alone, assuming that he fell in love with Nadine and her with him. This was the part of the curse that he had never really considered before Nadine's reappearance.

Whom was he kidding; he was already in love with her. Fingering the magic mirror on the table beside his favorite chair, he was tempted to see what she was up to, much like he had done as she had been growing up. He had witnessed her being kind and generous with her friends, family, and even that horrible stepfamily of hers. He watched her studying and reading and giving a speech -

while wearing a funny looking dress and hat - in front of a crowd of her classmates. He had even watched as Guy, the son of the enchantress who had cursed his family, had entered her life and tried to destroy everything.

Picking up the mirror, Richmond mumbled, "Show me Nadine."

Unaware that she was being observed not only by Richmond in his enchanted mirror but also by the two invisible servants that were standing out of the way, Nadine walked around the room touching the various different things scattered around her new space.

"This room is bigger than the first floor of my house," she whimpered, eyeing the massive four-poster bed through the doorway that led into a different room. Drawing in a deep breath, she gasped, "I have a sitting room." Spinning around, she caught a second glance at the two-person sofa, the various chairs and tables in the middle of the room, the fireplace, and the writing desk that was positioned to look out into one of the gardens.

Casting a final glance around the room, she slipped into the bedroom. After waking up in the room, she had already explored the massive space after Richmond had left her. There were only two more doors for her to examine and she headed over to the door on the left; it could only be a bathroom or a closet.

Throwing open the closet doors, Nadine walked into the massive walk-in. "This is bigger than my bedroom at home," she mumbled into the room filled with gowns, riding habits, and simpler dresses she thought might be day dresses.

Her jeans had gone missing overnight, forcing her into the dresses that lined the closet. Looking down, she wondered if Richmond had put her in the shift-like nightgown she was currently wearing or if there were servants around that she hadn't seen yet.

"I hate dresses!" she exclaimed into the closet as she reached for a light blue day dress and exited the closet. "Can I have my jeans back? Or a pair of pants period?" Maybe somebody would hear her request.

When nobody appeared to answer, she collapsed on the massive, four-poster bed with willowy curtains. Sinking into the mattress, she mumbled that she wished the bed were a bit firmer.

Slowly, Nadine noticed a change beneath her. Jumping up quickly, she began to spin around the room, looking at everything with a sense of panic on her face.

"Magic is real!" she exclaimed, suddenly looking around for the pants she had previously requested. Maybe they had appeared somewhere much like the mattress had firmed up underneath her.

"Well, how do you think you managed to cross over from what you would consider the real world into a fairy tale world?" Richmond asked from where he had been standing in her doorway.

"Not for fairy tales to be real!" she shouted at him, mostly from surprise, while holding up the blue dress in an attempt to cover the more revealing parts of her shift.

"You did not believe me before?" he mostly asked out of confusion. It wasn't often that people questioned him.

"Why should I?"

Richmond held a paw up and used a claw to point at his face. He didn't mention the fact that he was technically the Crown Prince until he was married and became King.

"Stage makeup," she dismissed. "They can do wonders with latex and makeup."

He raised an eyebrow at her.

"What do you expect?" Nadine snapped at him. "I just discovered that my boyfriend was cheating on me with my step-sister just so he could get his hands on some book. He froze me in place, twice, before disappearing into nothing right in the middle of my bedroom. Am I supposed to just accept it all with blind faith?"

Nodding his head, Richmond merely said, "Yes."

Sighing, she plopped back down on her now firmer mattress, ignoring the fact that she wasn't technically dressed. This shift covered more skin than swimsuits she had worn during the summer months at home.

Suddenly she realized that 'home' was no longer her home and all she wanted was one familiar thing. "I want my pants back," she wanted to cry.

Nadine glared at him when he began to laugh.

"Let me guess," Nadine sighed when he found her wandering the halls two hours later. "The West Wing is forbidden."

Richmond shrugged, "Why would it be?"

Turning to face him, she asked, "Is anything forbidden?"

"No. I'm not as barbaric as the original beast, despite my appearance."

"I never said you were."

"Look," he growled, "I ensured that you would know this story. Leave the metal rose alone and don't try to leave. The gates will not let you leave anyway and the forest will just turn you back towards the Castle."

"You don't have to growl at me!" Nadine hissed back.

"I would not growl if you would only listen to me!"

"You don't give me a chance! I ask a question and you growl at me." Closing her eyes, Nadine let out a sigh that startled Richmond and kept him from retorting. It gave her the chance to say, "I may not be from around here…"

"But you are," he interrupted, falling back into silence at her glare.

"I may not have grown up in the Enchanted Forest, but thanks to your generous gift when I was a child I grew up on fairy tales." Once again her expression caused Richmond to hesitate. She remembered that her fairy tale education had technically begun long before she had even met Richmond.

Finally, after watching the various expressions that passed over her face, he asked, "What is your point?"

"This tale we are in is Beauty and the Beast," she dryly reminded him.

"So?"

Hesitantly, she whispered, "I am supposed to fall in love with you and you with me in order to break this curse."

"And?" He didn't understand her point because he'd had decades to reconcile his reality to the tale.

She knew he wasn't asking a question when she continued, "And your lack of charm, lack of compassion, and arrogance is not going to accomplish that goal. You growl at the drop of a book. Get angry without reason..."

"It is not like you are much of a beauty yourself. Your hair alone..." Richmond began to insult her back; his pride pricked more than anything else.

"Give me your dagger," Nadine demanded as she pulled her hair into a low ponytail using the only rubber band she had brought with her.

"What?"

"I know you carry a dagger," she snapped. "Give it to me!"

"Why do you want my dagger?" Visions of her using it to stab him flashed through his mind.

"Dagger! Now!" The tears in her eyes contradicted her tone.

Handing it over, Richmond watched as she sliced through her hair just below her shoulders. It wasn't a great cut - the hair was longer on one side than the other - but it was considerably shorter than it had been in years.

Holding out the mass of hair, she shoved both hair and dagger towards him and took off at a run, not staying long enough to see if he grabbed for either object.

Staring at the hair and dagger on the floor, he sighed.

"That was badly done, Sir," a voice stated from behind him.

"I am aware of that," he growled. "Wait? How long have you been able to talk?"

"As long as Princess Nadine has been here," the formerly silent servant responded. "We would like her to not know that we can speak if possible." Taking an audible breath, he explained, "We do not want to frighten her."

All Richmond did was nod his head while staring at the clump of hair in his hand that he had picked up off of the floor, leaving the dagger behind. He actually liked her hair that long and wished he had not insulted her out of anger. Sadly, he was aware that everything she had said about him was true. That was one of the consequences of spending hundreds of years alone.

Richmond stared from the window while he watched Nadine pace in the garden. He had watched her shaking the gates in an attempt to get out, but it did not work. Instead, she paced like a caged animal, similar to how he had paced the gardens for the past three hundred and twenty years, thereabouts. He had lost track of time at one point. It would not take much for the spell to be broken and for the gates to let them pass: only her heart.

Words exchanged in anger still floated in the air. Silent servants passed it around in their own language developed over the years. In another hour everybody in the house would know the heartless things she had said to him and what he had said in response.

Heartless. Selfish. A jerk. A cold-hearted…a slam from below stopped that train of thought. A glance out the window told him that she had gone inside.

Minutes passed and he could hear her approach thanks to his supernatural hearing.

"I want to go home," she shouted, slamming his door shut behind her and causing him to wince. "I want out of this giant birdcage!"

Richmond mentally saw the bricks of her tower building themselves back into place. "You cannot leave," he mumbled, expecting a door and a lock to go up next.

"Why not?"

"Because the fairy tale is not complete." With that, the shutters over the tower window went into place. Within a day she had walled herself away from him.

"I don't want to be a part of any more fairy tales!" she shouted, the words rebounding off the walls. "I have lost my father and best friend because of a fairy tale. I lost my college scholarships because of a fairy tale. I lost my innocence because of a fairy tale. I want to go home, finally finish college, apply for a job, and teach middle school English." Sitting down hard in one of the nearby chairs, Nadine began to sob.

Tears were something that Richmond had never understood. He doubted that she wanted him to touch her. A nudge pushed him forward and he glared at where he assumed the servant was standing. A piece of cloth floated towards him, followed by another nudge.

"Here," he growled, unused to having to deal with the 'softer' emotions. "Please, do not cry. It is not like you will be stuck here forever."

She hiccupped, "I know this fairy tale; I have to fall in love with you…"

"How hard can it be? I am quite charming," he attempted to joke.

"…and you have to fall in love with me." Looking him in the eye, "You are emotionless and heartless; we'll be here forever."

"At least we will age slowly," he shrugged, fighting to get Nadine to laugh.

Nadine burst into tears and ran out of the room.

"What did I say?" he asked the servant, bewildered at her response.

If he could see the looks on the servants' faces, he would have been even more confused than he already was.

Chapter 10

A Gift

Richmond sat in his study fuming after Nadine had left him. The longer he reflected on the scene in the hallway, in his chambers, and everything she had said to him, the angrier he became.

He had faith in the tale; it had yet to let any of his forefathers down. He had no choice but trust that the Tradition would lead him in the right direction. The curse may suck, but it had a built-in soulmate clause that made things easier. Breaking the curse meant that he had to overcome the hundreds of years he was left alone with only invisible servants, a rose, and an enchanted mirror for company.

As much as he did not want to admit it, Nadine was right. He was an outright beast to her. He had years to deal with this, to use the mirror to watch her grow up, and she had only been there a couple of days.

The realization only frustrated him even more.

"Show me Nadine," he whispered to the mirror that sat next to the rose. His only choice was to ignore the fallen petal under the rose in favor of the mirror; Richmond did not want to acknowledge the fact that time was beginning to tick down.

He had no clue when the next one would fall.

Through the mirror, Richmond watched Nadine fling herself on one of the sitting room couches. "Are there no books in this entire castle?" she asked the ceiling. "A bookcase? A library? A nightstand with a lone book hidden away in a drawer?" As she began to groan and moan to the servants she didn't know were in the room, Richmond had an idea.

It took almost an hour to make certain that the room was in a decent - undestroyed - order. The last thing he wanted was for his plan to fall apart all because he had destroyed the library in a fit of rage. Reading had become an impossible task once his claws had begun to appear.

Once he had checked out the condition of the room, it took him some time to locate Nadine. Finally, after twenty minutes of hunting her down without the aid of the mirror, he located her in one of the outside gardens.

She could hear his approach. It would be nearly impossible not to hear the crunch of gravel beneath his paws.

After spending over an hour searching the castle for a pair of scissors to fix her hair, she realized that she had barely explored half of the castle. She had yet to locate a library as well. Her only option to preserve an ounce of her sanity was to head outside, lie out on a bench, and stare at the clouds.

Briefly, she considered remaining silent on her bench in the hopes that Richmond would walk on past without noticing her. Instead, she burst out in tears as soon as he turned the corner and looked directly at her. "I can't find any scissors," she managed to whimper through her hiccups. "Or books."

Holding out a 'hand', Richmond gestured for Nadine to follow him as he led her slowly back towards her room. "Let's go find the scissors first. There should be a mending basket somewhere in your room."

He hoped that one of the invisible servants bound to be following her would have heard his indirect request and had hurried off to deposit a mending basket - with scissors - in her sitting or dressing room.

Thirty minutes later, after evening out her impulsive haircut, Nadine didn't have a clue how to acknowledge Richmond, who had decided to hang out in her sitting room while she trimmed her hair.

Finally, "What is this place?" Nadine curiously asked him as she stared out her bedroom window. Something was darting around the castle that she could not quite get a clear glimpse of, but she had other questions pestering her.

"It is known as the Kingdom of Oublié to those who remember its existence," Richmond gruffly informed her.

"Forgotten?"

"What?"

"Oublié is French for forgotten."

Richmond snorted, the sound intensified by his beastly features. "How fitting. The Forgotten Kingdom."

Turning back to the window she whispered, "What's beyond Oublié?"

"The Enchanted Forest; the Land of Fairy Tales." He gave a one-shouldered shrug before adding, "Although, technically, every Kingdom is part of the Enchanted Forest. And there are a few other tales that have floating islands attached."

Straining her eyes, Nadine tried to see them. "How do you know?"

"There's a map," was all he said before turning to leave the room. Pausing at the doorway, he asked, "Coming?"

"Where?"

"To the Library," he nonchalantly answered her, even though he had originally tracked Nadine down in order to show her where the library was located.

Unable to tolerate the silence between them during the ridiculously long trek to the library, Nadine blurted out, "I'm adopted. I have no clue about who my birth parents are."

Richmond snorted his response. It seemed obvious to him at least where they were from.

"What?"

Holding back his mental eye roll, he answered her without looking backward to judge her reaction. "Your parents are from or attached to the Enchanted Forest."

"How do you know that?"

"Because you are here," he dryly answered her, having to remind himself that it had been a trying couple of days and she could not be expected to connect the dots concerning everything instantly.

"What does that mean?" Her frustrated tone caused him to look backward at her.

Carefully picking his words, the last thing Richmond wanted to do was frustrate her even further. "You are here, in my castle. This means quite a few things. According to this origin tale, you have two older sisters, possibly three brothers but that always varies from cursed generation to cursed generation, a father in trade…"

"My adoptive father owned a bakery," she interjected.

"That fits." He paused before adding, "This is not some Disney tale - whatever that is - so something dark and sinister is bound to happen." Richmond hesitated as he wondered where the word 'Disney' had appeared from in his vocabulary.

Nodding her head, Nadine scanned her memory on the various Beauty and the Beast tales she had found. "So either Brother's Grimm or that French version that I can remember the name of the author only about half of the time." She paused. "Probably French because your kingdom means forgotten in French."

Richmond shrugged his response. Some of the things he knew, that he should not know, puzzled him.

"What?"

Not answering her question about his response, he opened the Library doors and guided her inside instead. Giving her a moment to sigh over the massive shelves filled with books already written and not-yet written, he waited before giving her his answer.

"This is the Enchanted Forest where French, German, English, and who knows what other tales are meshed together." Stopping in place, he turned around and told her to follow him.

"Where are we going?"

He was silent until he led her even further into the library. "This section," he pointed, "contains every single tale founded by and connected to this forsaken place. You see British authors, and Canadian authors, and American authors, among the French, German, and other languages." Holding up his claws, he added, "I cannot read them anymore, but this library adds them anyway. Although I did manage to get through several of these shelves before I couldn't anymore."

Tilting her head, Nadine realized something. "You enjoyed reading," she blurted out.

Ignoring her comment, he added, "You could be a merchant's daughter or a royal daughter; I can't tell you."

Especially since the servants did not want her to know that they could talk yet.

Richmond started to leave the room, leaving Nadine to stare at the books. "Somewhere is also genealogies to the families, but I do not know where they are shelved either; I never had any interest in them. Based on our genealogies our story could go in any direction."

"Meaning?"

"Meaning if you are a Red Riding Hood descendant a huntsman might come to kill me."

Nadine started to laugh, "But this is a fairy tale!"

"And not all of them ended happily." He started to leave, pausing in the doorway, "And you did arrive wearing a red hooded thing." When he did leave, she was staring blankly at the shelves, uncertain where she should begin.

Chapter 11

Family Trees

Running her fingers along the shelves, Nadine was careful to keep her fingers off the spines unless she was examining a book. After three days, she had yet to find the genealogy section. It was critical that she find that section; she was dying to know what kingdom she was from originally.

Nobody had to tell her. She was in the middle of a 'quest' to help the Crown Prince of the Forgotten Kingdom. There was no possible way that she was not a princess. It was the only explanation she could give on why she had been sent to live with her father and mother. *Adoptive father and mother*, she always had to correct herself mentally.

Moreover, that knowledge terrified her.

Without that genealogy, she had no clue if she was a Crown Princess or merely a Spare Princess. Although realistically, when she took the time to think about it, her being a Spare was the more likely scenario since she was in the middle of a tale with a Crown Prince.

She had done enough digging to realize that the female line rules some kingdoms and the male line ruled others.

"Where is that book?" she hissed, leaving another section of books and entering the next.

A thump at one of the desks in the middle of the room caught her attention. Moving around the shelving and peering cautiously in the middle of the room, Nadine noticed a book sitting on the desk.

A book that previously hadn't been there before with a tray of food sitting next to it.

She wasn't surprised by the food; somebody had frequently left her food whenever she missed a meal. Nadine expected Richmond to come storming into the library demanding that she join him for meals, but he had yet to make those commands.

Truthfully, Nadine was surprised that he hadn't made those demands already.

A knock on the door caught her attention as she contemplated popping a grape in her mouth. She didn't have a clue where the grapes or other fruits on this tray had come from. The weather wasn't suitable for grapes or cherries and she had yet to see a greenhouse in her exploring.

Granted, she had spent the last three days in the library.

"Come in," Nadine called out, not surprised when Richmond entered the room.

"You did not come to lunch," he pointed out, eyeing the food on the table. "I was worried."

"You knew I was in here," she pointed out. "You could have come and escorted me to the dining room."

Raising an eyebrow, he looked at her before asking, "You do not know where the dining room is?"

"Oh, I know where it is, but I've been so busy looking for this book," she finished with a grumble, pointing at the book on the table. "Then, just now in fact, I asked for the book and the next thing I know I hear it hitting this desk."

"Are you sure it is the right book?"

"Enchanted Forest Genealogy is written across it." Nadine eyed the book a little longer, noting the subtitle, *The History of the Kingdoms of the Enchanted Forest*.

"And you have not opened it."

Toying with the bite-sized sandwiches, she hesitated to answer him.

"Nervous?" he asked instead.

Picking up a sandwich that seemed unfamiliar to her, Nadine popped it into her mouth. "Chicken salad?"

"My cook likes to add raisins," he commented. "And paprika."

"That's why it looks so red." She grabbed another one, trying to decide if she liked it or not.

Richmond pretended to tap the cover of the book with his claw. When Nadine jerked it away from him, he started to laugh. "Open the book already."

"Do you see how thick this thing is?" she hissed. "At least six inches!"

"Open the book," he commanded.

Huffing, "Fine," she opened the book and noticed that there was a table of contents. "What?"

Shaking his head, Richmond pulled out the chair next to where Nadine was standing. "This is a magical book. It adds new additions with minimal effort on the owner's part. Each kingdom has one of these in their Hall of Tales."

"Yours was in your library…" she pointed out, drawing out the end of her sentence until it seemed as if she hadn't finished the sentence at all.

Richmond looked at the room around him. Three floors of books with multiple freestanding shelves scattered around the room. There were several alcoves, much like the Kingdom's Tales alcoves, were formed by these freestanding shelves.

"Where did you start?"

Pulling out the chair next to Richmond, Nadine hesitated to admit that she didn't start with the Kingdom's Tales.

"Nadine?"

She shoved another sandwich in her mouth instead of answering. Tomato and turkey.

"You did not start where I suggested, did you?"

"I couldn't find it again," she admitted around the sandwich in her mouth.

"And you did not ask for help?" he asked, raising an eyebrow in the process.

Swallowing, "I'm used to doing things by myself. I never get to ask for help," she confessed.

"Then you need to get over that," Richmond growled, grabbing one of the roast beef sandwiches from the platter. "We know how this story ends," he stated, pointing out something that they both had avoided ever since Nadine had chopped off her hair in a fit of anger.

Quietly she asked him, uncertain if she wanted to know the answer, but knowing she needed it, "Has the time ever run out on one of your relatives?"

Shaking his head, Richmond told her all that she needed to know. "If it ever fails then it will…" he hesitated. "It will probably be the end of my family line."

Getting the feeling he wasn't telling her something, Nadine cocked her head to the side. She wanted to ask him what he was holding back, but something kept her silent. If he ever wanted to tell her then he would. Keeping her mouth closed was something she'd mastered after her father died.

Waiting for a beat to see if he added anything else, Nadine realized that she could discover the answer herself. "Okay, fine," she sighed, pulling the book towards her.

Her family history would be in this book, but so would his.

Opening the book, she was surprised to discover that there was a reference guide at the beginning of the book. "Huh." Although, she thought, it made sense that there would be a table of contents, even if it did magically change when the book made adjustments.

Shaking his head, Richmond grabbed another roast beef sandwich, but he waited before eating it.

"Where do I start?" Nadine whispered as she started flipping through the various stories referenced in the guide. The list of tales alone was overwhelming.

"With the obvious," Richmond pointed out. "You entered this place wearing a red hoodie."

Nodding her head at his point, she added, "I still want my hoodie back. That was quite comfortable."

"It will not match your dresses and skirts." He wondered if she would comment on his manners if he jammed the sandwich in his mouth whole. Noticing that she was distracted, he did exactly that.

"I hate dresses and skirts," she snapped. "I want my pants back as well."

Shrugging, he delivered the bad news. "There are only a few family lines where pants are acceptable. Little Red Riding Hood's line is not one of them."

"Fine," Nadine grumbled, flipping through the guide to discover where the Little Red Riding Hood's family tree was located. "There's sixteen tales connected to this one story!" she exclaimed once she reached the right pages.

Peering over her shoulder, Richmond noticed that there were Goldilocks, Alice in Wonderland, Peter Pan, Sleeping Beauty, and so many others listed. "And the Little Red Riding Hood family tree will only tell you what branch married into what family."

"Of course this can't be easy," Nadine mumbled.

Richmond paused, thinking for a moment. Finally, he stated, "This could be your first quest."

"Quest?"

Taking a deep breath, he eyed the last roast beef sandwich on the platter. Nodding his head firmly, aware that he couldn't just reach for that sandwich and jam it into his mouth as well, he began to explain. "Every royal has a quest, or a series of quests. It is usually three trials that they have to experience before they can be deemed worthy of whatever challenge it was that they were facing."

"And discovering my family line is a quest?"

Pointing at the book with his claw, he reminded her that the genealogy was six inches thick and she had sixteen tales to search. "Possibly."

"No other hints to help me narrow it down? Maybe something about my name or hair color or anything?"

"There are so many blondes in these tales," he admitted. "It does eliminate the non-blonde stories."

"I'm not a blonde," she pointed out.

Shaking his head, Richmond held back his laughter at her denial. Had she not looked in a mirror since cutting her hair? "You are too a blonde."

"No," she protested, "I'm what is called a dishwater blonde. A mix of blonde and light brown…" she trailed off as she glanced at her reflection in one of the serving trays. "How did that happen?"

Richmond shrugged, "The Tradition."

Having encountered multiple references of the Tradition in her readings already, all Nadine did was let out a long sigh. "What is the point of my hair color changing? I like my brown hair. In fact, I wish it had been a few shades darker."

"It is probably one of those factors that are intended to be clues. Reality, your mother is probably a blonde and your father a brunette. Unless your father is the ruler of the kingdom in which case he would be the blonde."

Narrowing her eyes, Nadine thought for a really long moment. Nothing she could currently do would undo what the magic had done to her appearance. Later, she would try wishing for her natural hair color back.

Finally, she asked, "But these are factors that could help narrow things down, right?"

Richmond only nodded his head, having stuffed that last roast beef sandwich in his mouth while she had been thinking.

"You are always hungry, aren't you?" she asked him, tilting her head curiously as she examined him. She thought twice about commenting on his lack of manners.

"Almost," he admitted. "Roast beef is my favorite."

"At home," she slowly stated, "I mostly had peanut butter and jelly. It was easy to make and take with me." Looking sadly at the remaining sandwiches. "Where I worked served some delicious chicken salad sandwiches on a croissant roll cut in half. There was also some oven-roasted turkey breast with Swiss cheese on sourdough bread." She sighed at the memory of her favorite sandwiches. "Normally, people ordered chicken with sourdough, but I liked the substitution."

"You are stalling now," Richmond interrupted, even though he kept a mental note of her favorites.

"Maybe a little," she admitted. "I need some paper."

Getting up, he showed her where the paper and writing equipment was stashed.

Eyeing the modern ink pen oddly, she looked over at where Richmond was hovering. "Up-to-date pens?"

"The castle keeps up," he shrugged, "mostly."

"Then where are the modern lights?"

"They will appear once the curse is broken. Then, hopefully, my scouts will return with more advanced technology." He grinned at the thought. "Although, now that I think about it, some sections of the castle do have modern lights that are designed to fit into the design of the castle."

"At least there are modern bathrooms," she admitted. "I'd be lost otherwise."

Grinning a toothy grin, Richmond added, "I am thankful for hot water and showers, although it takes a while for me to dry off."

Holding the paper and pens to her chest, Nadine shyly smiled at the beast in front of her. They were getting along!

Walking back over to the book, she spread out a few sheets of paper and started copying out the tales she could be connected to out on one of the pages.

On another page she listed attributes that could connect her to those stories.

Blonde hair

Blue Eyes

Red hoodie

Name ???

"Could my name narrow things down?" she asked Richmond, turning to look at him.

Tilting his head, a habit he had picked up from Nadine, he scratched his head. "Possibly," he determined. "Some families carry down characteristics of their names or their tales. Most of the Sleeping Beauty like names their children after flowers or the dawn. Lots of Roses, Dawns, and Auroras."

"So not Sleeping Beauty," she concluded, marking out the story from her list.

"Cinderella stories tend to have Ellas and Eleanors. Lots of E names if I recall correctly."

Nadine flipped to that story to confirm his theory. Seeing all of the E names, she quickly marked through that possibility."

Slowly they narrowed stories down. Dark-haired princesses like those found in Snow White's line - Nadine did breathe a sigh of relief when she eliminated that possibility. It took a lot longer than either of them expected.

Finally, Nadine flipped through the pages and ran her finger carefully down the family tree.

Snapping the book closed, she leaned back in her chair and closed her eyes. "I have two older sisters and a younger brother. My mother is the Queen of Wonderland." At the discovery, she felt something shift into place inside her.

Chapter 12

Inconvenient Reality

Richmond closed his eyes and tried to block out the sight, and sounds, of Nadine wandering around the estate. The problem with closing his eyes, his hearing and sense of smell improved.

Every time he thought he had escaped her scent of vanilla and cinnamon, he caught another whiff of it. Her presence haunted him while her lack of appearance taunted him.

Things were easier when she had been hiding out in the library.

Even right then he could tell that she was trying to creep up on him. She was not very subtle about it, although if he had human hearing then she might have succeeded. Human hearing and a human sense of smell that is.

"Nadine," he greeted her, not even turning around.

"I was trying to surprise you," she pouted, walking around to face him.

"You thought surprising a man that is mostly a beast was a good idea. I could have clawed you or…"

Rolling her eyes, Nadine started to walk backward away from you. "You also heard me."

"I smelled you first," he admitted.

"So it was unlikely that you would claw me to death," she pointed out.

Shaking his head, Richmond opted to follow her instead of replying. "You came looking for me?"

"There's nobody else to talk to here," she admitted.

"Well, we are in the middle of the hallway," he pointed out. "Not many people hang out in hallways."

"There is nobody else in this entire place," she nearly repeated, ignoring his joke. "There's nobody else to talk to here," she did repeat.

"What am I? Chopped liver?" he growled, disappointed that she was seeking him out because she did not have a choice.

Nadine looked at him curiously. "Chopped liver?"

"What?"

"I'm just wondering where you heard that phrase from."

Richmond paused as he thought about it. "I really do not know," he finally conceded after a long moment. "It just came out."

Shrugging, she dismissed it as one of those things that the forest and enchantment provided its denizens. Like indoor plumbing and other technical advances that appeared despite the kingdom being isolated for generations.

"Come on," Richmond sighed. He was tempted to take her hand, but it would be more like her wrapping her hand around a claw. "Let's go."

"Where are we going?"

"It's a surprise."

Nadine let him lead her through the castle before they emerged out on the backside of the gardens. If she had thought that the library was impressive, the stables blew that room away.

"Are there any horses?"

"Not yet," he admitted to her. "They are terrified of me at the moment."

Tilting her head in concession, Nadine accepted his point. That was until she saw the bucket filled with oats hovering in one of the corners, barely moving. Looking around, she also noticed a bridle that was floating in the air and not hanging on the racks with the other bridles. Then it was a horse brush.

"Ummm," Nadine hesitated, her head beginning to spin.

She'd been at the estate for a little over a week and didn't know why she didn't realize it before. It wasn't magic that was doing things around the castle.

"The servants are invisible," she stated.

Richmond froze in place. "What?" was the only thing he could think to say. He had hoped that she wouldn't realize that tiny piece of information.

"The servants are invisible," she repeated. "The servants are invisible."

He could tell that Nadine was having difficulty processing this information.

"Why didn't you tell me?"

"It did not seem necessary," Richmond replied. "They are just servants."

Her face tightened, lips pursed. Suddenly, he realized that he had said the wrong thing. "What?"

"They are just servants?" she hissed. "Are you kidding me?" Bumping into him, she left the stables and stormed away.

Richmond stood there, stunned. "What did I say?"

The three servants who had witnessed the exchange remained silent, even though, as Richmond very well knew, they could now talk. They weren't aware that one of the kitchen errand boys had fallen asleep in one of the stables.

"You called us just servants," he piped up. If Richmond could see what the others could see, he would see a little boy about eight years old peering over the edge of the stall door. "I thought we were more than that to you."

"You are," Richmond replied, feeling confused.

"But we are just servants," the boy threw back at him.

Somebody else spoke up then, "We have been with you for hundreds of years. Frozen in time while getting to watch you age."

"I really do not want to be eight years old anymore."

"And all we are to you," a third voice added, "are servants."

"We do not matter," the fourth, and last, voice concluded.

Richmond shrunk into himself as he realized what his careless words implied. "I did not mean it like that."

"But that is how everybody is taking it."

"And," the kitchen boy added, "Princess Nadine's family treated her as if she was just a servant."

Nadine barely heard Richmond walking into the library. She knew it was him. Who else could it possibly be? Even though the servants were merely invisible and not non-existent, she knew enough to know that they wouldn't make any noise when they entered rooms.

"My stepmother and stepsiblings treated me like I was a servant. They didn't care an iota about me unless it meant that I couldn't do what they wanted me to do." She leaned further back against the chair she was sitting in and closed her eyes.

"There was this one time," she added, "that I was sick. I probably should have been in the hospital, but Heather didn't want to take me. I was forced to clean the house for a party she had planned. I was so sick that I ended up throwing up over everything in my room and was stuck in bed far longer than I would have been if I had gotten the rest and care I needed in the first place." Shaking her head, Nadine concluded, "Heather had never planned a party. She just wanted the house cleaned."

Richmond stood nearby, stunned to hear what Nadine's life had been like during the times he had not spied on her through the magic mirror. He had seen her reading and studying, but never slaving away. He admitted to himself that he probably should have watched her more over the last several years.

"When my father died," Nadine continued, not looking at Richmond as she fell into her memories, "my stepmother sold the bakery even though she didn't have the legal right. By the time the ownership papers were found, she had spent all of the money on the mortgage she had taken out on the house without my father's permission. I don't know how she did it. Mortgaging the house required his signature, but she was able to do it anyway. Maybe she had a sneaky lawyer in her pocket and forged my father's signature. The bakery…"

Richmond caught the way she choked whenever she mentioned that bakery. "What about the bakery?"

"That was left to me in his will. I don't know if he knew I would be transported here when I turned twenty-one. That day really sucked." For the first time, she looked up at him before saying, "The day that I arrived here was my twenty-first birthday."

"That makes sense," he admitted. "Happy belated birthday." He had already suspected as much, but did not say anything at the time. Princess Portals appeared on their twenty-first birthdays.

"Thanks." She went back to looking at the flickering flames in the fireplace. "I'd put in a full day at the bakery, the bakery that should have been mine, and I come home and discover the person I had been dating for nearly a year had been cheating on me with my stepsister." Nadine started to laugh. "He used her for sex and he used me for the book."

"Guy," Richmond growled.

"Yeah."

"Blonde hair?"

"Yeah."

"He is a descendant of one of the fairies that had cursed my family," Richmond admitted. "His name is really Gaubert."

Nadine let out a snort of laughter at Richmond's news. "No wonder he called himself Guy."

"He has a sister. Angelique. She is vastly different from her brother."

"Huh," was all Nadine said for a long moment. "I knew an Angela when I was working at the bakery. Sometimes she didn't seem quite human."

"Unless she had transformed herself so that Gaubert would not recognize her, it is doubtful that Angela and Angelique were the same person," Richmond stated.

They dropped the conversation about how Nadine had been treated growing up, but it was enough for Richmond to start thinking about how he treated his own servants. He really did not want her to begin comparing her stepfamily to him and start finding similarities.

Chapter 13

Research

Nadine, realizing that she knew nothing about her family, found herself back in the library. It did not take Richmond long to figure out where she had taken to hiding.

"What are you doing?" he asked her once he had located her in one of the book alcoves.

She held *Alice in Wonderland* up for him to see. "I thought I would read up on my family. It's been years since I read this."

"That is a good start," Richmond stated, finding a place to settle on the floor.

He lamented the fact that he currently did not fit into any of the chairs in the library. Before Nadine arrived it did not matter; while he could get lost between the shelves when he was younger, once the transformation began and his claws began to form the escape that the library provided evaporated.

He missed reading.

By clearing her throat, Nadine regained his attention. "A lot of these places, according to my readings, follow the traditions of their stories."

"Things evolve," Richmond interjected.

"What do you mean?"

Closing his eyes, Richmond considered his choices. He could lead Nadine over to where the books she needed were or he could ask one of the servants to do it. A few days ago he would have asked one of the library attendants to retrieve the necessary tomes. Today...

Standing up, he held out his hand to Nadine. "This way. There are some more books you need to be aware of."

"There are?"

"I am afraid so. Royal protocols, the Traditions of the various tales. Some of the story islands, like the Wonderland island, continue on without starting all over again. Other story islands are on a repeat loop, but I am not certain which ones. One of these books will tell you."

Nadine studied Richmond carefully before asking, "How do you know this?"

"I did not always look like this, or have these," he held up his claws. "The servants could not talk until you returned here and started everything rolling, so I was left alone to my own devices. I rode the horses until they turned invisible..."

"When did that happen?" she interrupted him.

"I started changing when I was seventeen; you would have had your thirteenth birthday when that happened." He thought for a moment before adding, "It all developed slowly. The horns were first, then the hair, fangs, and finally the claws formed."

"When did they show up?" she asked, curious. With his head down, he didn't notice that her hand had reached out towards him.

"Last year," he admitted, not seeing when Nadine pulled her hand back.

"So," she drew out, "you've gone a year without reading a book?"

"Pretty much, but before that I had over three hundred years in this library. I was aware whenever a new book was added to the shelves, but that might be because somebody put it on one of the tables for me…" he trailed off, realizing just how much the servants did for him.

Nadine noticed the growing realization on Richmond's face.

Turning to scan the shelves, she looked at the titles that lined the small bookcase.

Royal Protocols

A Guide to the Enchanted Forest and Its

    Surrounding Kingdoms

Classic Stories and Their Traditions

Fairy Tales and The Tradition

"Richmond?" Nadine asked after reading the author names on the binding.

"Yes?"

"Most of these books share a last name."

"Probably because they were written by the same person." Richmond pulled one of them off the shelves and handed it to her. "This one should be the most helpful." He eyed the shelves again and handed her two more books. Then, without thinking, he grabbed the last book and placed it on her stack. "Yeah, you might want to read all four of them."

Shaking her head, Nadine shelved the books back into their places for safekeeping. "Thanks," she smiled at him. "I'm going to start here," she grabbed *Classic Stories and Their Traditions* off the shelf. "I can check out the stuff about Wonderland first."

Chapter 14

Angelique

Try as she might, Angela could not figure out where Nadine was in this vast kingdom. No amount of scouring or magical seeing could pinpoint the Wonderland Princess' location. This told her that Nadine had to be in one of the cursed kingdoms.

She had to find Nadine before Gaubert did.

Her older brother had been corrupted by their mother at a young age. Their mother, an enchantress, was part of the line that cursed the second generation of Richmond's familial line. The original curse was a redemption curse that a long-forgotten aunt had created to temper the arrogance of Prince Adam from the original tale.

One of her sisters was the evil fairy that had cursed Princess Aurora of the Roschen Kingdom.

While their background was a mix of good and evil, Angela's mother had been disappointed that her daughter had taken after the good side of their family tree. But really, what did she expect would happen when she named her daughter Angelique?

Angela didn't even want to consider what her mother thought when she had named Gaubert.

Angela had recognized his blonde head the moment he walked into the bakery and knew that nothing good was going to come of it.

She had been right.

And now she had no clue where Nadine was at except somewhere in the Enchanted Forest.

Angela, originally Angelique, had proclaimed herself Nadine's fairy godmother. After figuring out Gaubert's - she would never call him Guy - plan to take down the Enchanted Forest, she quit her job at the bakery.

It felt good walking up to Marge and saying, "I quit."

It felt even better when Marge protested because they were already short-staffed with both Nadine - not that they remembered Nadine - and Meg no longer working there.

It felt great when Angela cataloged every single bad and unprofessional way Marge treated her employees in front of the customers. Even more so when they clapped. It was like a scene from a romantic comedy when the main character told off whomever it was that kept pushing her down.

It took her another hour to locate the nearest portal to the Enchanted Forest. It took nothing to check to see who all had entered and exited the portal and closing it behind her to potentially halt her brother's process of returning to their mother. Provided he had not already found the portal and entered it. It was a possibility. The longer she had remained in this world the harder it was to perform her scouring magic. All she knew for certain was that Nadine had passed through the portal.

Unless Gaubert knew how to cloak himself, he must still be on the other side of the portal. Hopefully.

Portals involved very special magic. A Princess' tracker could only open and close the portals twice; once to drop off a princess and once to retrieve her. While fairies and witches, in theory, could open a portal, they don't have the necessary magic to do so. Sometimes portals opened because a Princess needed to pass through.

Closing that portal meant creating more obstacles for Gaubert. Unless he had already passed through. Shaking her head, Angela figured she would deal with Gaubert if he ever appeared. Right now she needed to find Nadine.

Looking into the pool of water she was using as a scouring source, she splashed the puddle in frustration. It was as if Nadine had been forgotten in…

"Forgotten…" she trailed off, repeating part of her thoughts. "The Forgotten Kingdom. Of course Nadine would be in Oublié." Nobody could see into Oublié as long as the curse held.

Pulling out a notebook from her bag, Angela flipped through the pages. She had read a fiction book about fairy godmothers - a book by an author with a car name - and the Fairy Godmother had a spell that sped up travel through the forests. It had inspired her to attempt to create a similar spell.

"All Forests Are One Spell," she mumbled to herself as she flipped through the pages. It was unoriginal, using the name of the spell from the book, but she couldn't think of anything else that explained it any better.

Finding the spell, she quickly cast it, uncertain how close to the spell could get her to the castle. Even if it couldn't get her inside the gates, she could still run interference if Gaubert ever appeared.

Truthfully, Angela had no clue if a spell she had created in the other world would even work in the Enchanted Forest.

Chapter 15

The Gates

Straining her ears to listen carefully for the sound of Richmond's breathing, Nadine closed her eyes. She learned early that he had mastered the art of blending into the shadows, even the shadows she didn't expect him to be able to fit into. In order to better rely on her hearing, she discovered that closing her eyes would help improve that sense.

If she ever wanted to make her escape, she would have to be careful about it. The knowledge that the servants were actually invisible added to her caution. Being unable to hear them made it even more difficult.

"Is there anybody nearby?" she quietly asked, her voice barely over a whisper. "Lift up one of the candles on the table if there is anybody in the room. Please."

Nadine couldn't see the three servants scattered around the front hallway polishing the unused candleholders. The candles that were on the tables were merely there for decoration. There had once been electric lights in the candle holders, lights that looked like candles and the flames, but the servants had too many issues replacing the lightbulbs that they had taken out the bulbs and decorative candles and replaced them with real candles.

Electric lighting magically went up on the ceilings and walls the next day, much to the unheard grumbling that these modern fixtures took away from the classic look inside the castle. Even if they were easier to clean. It was one of the many changes the servants had to adjust to since Richmond had begun to change and when Nadine arrived.

Nobody, and no candles, moved.

"Okay," Nadine sighed. "If there is anybody in here, I'm just going to the gates. I noticed somebody was down there. I'm not leaving. I might bring her back if I can, but I am not leaving. Please, don't let Richmond disturb us or come to the wrong conclusions. That is if you can talk. I haven't heard anybody talking before, and it would be nice if somebody would talk to me, but I understand why you wouldn't…" Nadine caught herself rambling and stopped talking. "Anyway, I will be back. I'm not trying to escape. I swear."

A deep voice from the top of the staircase replied, "That is good to know."

Nadine released a deep sigh as she turned around to face Richmond. "There you are," she tried to play it off.

"Do not tell me that you had been looking everywhere for me," he interjected before she could say more. "We both know you were trying to sneak out."

"I was doing no such thing," she unsuccessfully lied.

"Then why were you telling the poor servants to reassure me that you would be back? Why were you looking around trying to hide and trying to make certain that nobody was around to see you escape through that door?" Richmond's attempt at raising an eyebrow was not as successful as he wanted to believe.

"I…" Nadine hesitated. "I…"

"Exactly," Richmond replied, crossing his arms across his chest.

Taking a deep breath, she blurted out, "I saw Angela outside the gate. I was going to go down there and talk to her."

"I will go with you," he insisted.

"No!" the protest burst out. "I have to tell her about you first."

Chuckling, Richmond shook his head. "If Angela knows enough about how to leave your adoptive world and land at the base of my gates in a kingdom that most do not remember and many cannot travel more than ten miles into, then I am fairly certain she already knows about me."

"I haven't seen my best friend in weeks."

"Two weeks. You have barely been here two weeks."

"It feels like forever."

Richmond shook his head. "Look, Princess…" He paused when he recognized the bewildered expression on her face.

Nadine tilted her head in confusion as him referencing her title. It was the first time anybody had done so and it sounded odd to her. "Princess?"

"That is what you are, is it not?"

Thinking about it for a moment, "Yes, but…"

"Okay then," Richmond nodded his head.

"It sounds odd hearing it aloud." Nadine hadn't taken a moment to acknowledge the fact that she was an actual princess. Fundamentally, she knew it. Fundamentally, she knew that she would be called 'Princess' someday, but Richmond had called her Nadine so many times she never considered herself a princess.

Just as she never considered the fact that he had a title of his own.

"What is your title? Prince or King?"

"It is complicated," he answered her.

"How is it complicated?"

"Because I do not expect you to call me by my title."

"But you just called me by mine."

"Because you were acting like a stubborn princess."

"When am I not being stubborn?"

"Stubborn and determined are two different things."

"Stubborn and determined are two different sides of the exact same coin."

"Then I want to see this coin."

"It's a figure of speech!" Nadine retorted, throwing her arms and hands out in a frustrated gesture of 'are you kidding me?'

"You know I do not know very many of your figures of speeches."

"It's a metaphor. You know about metaphors."

One by one, the servants disappeared while the pair did their usual bickering back and forth. Even though Nadine and Richmond couldn't see them, they still wanted to give the pair some privacy.

The last thing they heard was Nadine saying something about contractions and how Richmond needed to learn how to use them if he didn't want to sound so formal and stuffy all of the time.

It took thirty minutes of 'arguing' before Nadine made her way down towards the gates where Angela was waiting. After five minutes of discussing it, Richmond had finally agreed to give Nadine a few minutes to explain the situation with Angela. Nadine had agreed to give Richmond a signal before he could join him.

It didn't take him long to explain that he needed to be at the gate in order for it to open long enough for Angela to enter.

"You weren't there when…"

"You did not enter through the gate," Richmond interjected.

"What are you talking about? Of course I…"

"The portal you came out of dropped you out on this side of the gates."

"No," she protested. "The gate opened for me and shut again right after I ran through it."

"That's impossible," Richmond argued. "That gate never opens without me."

"It opened for me. I can still hear Guy banging on the gates trying to get in."

"But I saw you…"

"Richmond!" Nadine interrupted him. "The gates opened for me. You found me in the garden at the front door." She drew in a breath before adding, "Besides, if Angela entered the same portal then wouldn't she be on this side of the gates?"

"Not necessarily. The portals might be set in stone in the mortal world, but they can move around in the Enchanted Forest. Some Royal Trackers can create portals, but they are limited on how many they can create between the mortal world and the fairy tale world."

Nadine started to think aloud, "So Angela can enter the same portal I did, but come out anywhere in the Enchanted Forest."

"Right, which means she probably came out on the outskirts of Oublié."

So, when Nadine finally made it to the gate where Angela was waiting the first question she asked was, "How did you get here?"

"I entered the portal in the state park near our town," Angela started. "I also closed it behind me before Guy could follow."

"He already followed me through," Nadine mumbled. "I think he's been trying to get past the gates ever since." She drew in a deep breath before adding, "I know he's your brother. Richmond told me."

"Is he as beastly as the rumors say?" Angela whispered, glancing behind Nadine towards the estate.

"What rumors?"

"Fangs. Horns. Claws?"

"And lots of hair, but he doesn't yell as much as the movies suggest. Except at me, but it's more of a debating argument than angry yelling. I don't think he knows how to temper his voice yet." Nadine glanced behind her. "Actually, he'll be here soon. He's one of the few people who can open this gate."

"You didn't enter through the gate?"

"That's apparently up for debate depending on who you ask. I was so frantic after the scene with Gaubert…"

"So you know everything."

"I don't know how you ended up on the good side."

Angela promised to tell her the story about her mother later. Instead, knowing their time was limited, she pointed towards the gates. "Have you looked at these? Really looked at these?"

Shaking her head, Nadine admitted that she had spent more time in the library and inside the estate than she did outside. Taking a step back, she noticed the rust, tarnish, and other grime that masked the gold plating. "What am I looking at?"

"Take a few more steps back."

A deep voice from behind her stated, "It is a man and a woman, facing different directions."

Angela took a deep breath, more out of surprise from his sudden appearance than his physical appearance, before she replied. "Your Highness," she curtsied.

"Please do not curtsy before me," Richmond corrected Angela. "I am not used to it and it seems weird. Please, call me Richmond."

Nadine cleared her throat. "You called me 'Princess' earlier."

"You were being stubborn and I was teasing you," he retorted.

Angela, still on her side of the gate, started grinning. It was only a matter of time.

After a long moment, she cleared her throat, "This gate is not the original gate."

"What?"

"How do you know this?" Richmond incidentally confirmed.

Angela tilted her head. Out of the three of them, she expected him to see the magic surrounding the gates. "You can't see it?"

"See what?"

"The magic surrounding the gates," she pointed out. "That's how I knew I couldn't open them myself."

Shaking his head, Richmond stared at the gates, "I don't see anything." He missed Nadine giving him a quick glance as she noticed he had dropped some of his formality that they had been 'arguing' over in the entryway of the castle.

"Then how do you know that these aren't the original gates?" Angela asked, breaking Nadine's astonishment at Richmond's use of a contraction.

Snorting, he answered smartly, "I saw them before my curse changed them."

"Fair enough," was all Angela had to say about it. "Anyway," she gestured towards the gate. "Can I have a little help?"

"Right. Of course," Richmond nodded his head. He opened the palm of his hand and pressed it over the rose engraving in the center of the gate. Within seconds the gates spread.

Grabbing her bag, Angela darted through the gates and onto the castle grounds quickly, before the gates closed.

Chapter 16

The Garden

"Hey," Angela popped her head into the library. "There you are!"

She hurried into the room, pulled Nadine up, and pulled her out of the room.

"Hey!" Nadine protested. "I was studying protocols!" The section about speaking formally had her rolling her eyes.

"You need a break, too. And nothing you will say will change my mind," Angela softly snapped. "For the past three days, you have been spending more and more time in the library reading those books."

"Richmond reads them with me," Nadine smiled.

Stopping before the staircase, Angela turned and faced her friend. "And you need a break." Leading Nadine the rest of the way, she didn't say anything or drop any clues about where they were going.

Angela had already gone out and explored bits and pieces of the castle and the grounds while attempting to get to know the weaknesses in their surroundings. She wouldn't know how to protect the castle if she couldn't determine how Gaubert was going to go about scaling the magical fortress.

In her explorations, she discovered something that she doubted Nadine was aware of in one of the gardens on the backside of the castle. Especially since her friend had spent so much time in the library.

Nadine said nothing until Angela pulled her outside the castle through a servants' door and into the back gardens. "I'm not supposed to be in here."

"Why not?"

"So I don't damage the rose," she stated as if it was obvious.

Laughing, "If the little dragons flying about can't damage that rose than I doubt you can." Rolling her eyes, she added, "Besides, Richmond has the rose locked away in his room and this isn't the rose garden that you first saw."

"Little dragons?" It was obvious that Nadine had never entered the garden, or heard the second part of Angela's comment. Instead, the mini dragons had caught Nadine's undivided attention.

Angela waved her hand, pointing out the dragons that were barely a foot long hovering over the flowers as if they were dragonflies.

Stunned, Nadine took several steps into the garden. Watching them dart around her and landing on flowers and shrubbery, she asked, "Are they normally this little?"

"No. And there aren't usually this many of them." Angela joined her friend inside the garden. "I have a suspicion that when the castle was frozen in time, these dragons were babies. Everything else was frozen in time, but the dragons…"

"They multiplied," Nadine smiled, counting at least twenty miniature dragons that fluttered around them.

"They probably did multiply," Angela agreed. "They would still age, but stay the same size."

"Once this curse is broken do you think that they'll remain tiny or begin to grow?"

Angela pondered this question for a moment. "I really don't know. They are so used to these gardens that if they did grow to their full sizes I don't think this estate would survive. They are sleeping in that abandoned tower, and normally these castle towers are only designed for one dragon per estate. If they do become full size, there will be a fight over who gets to stay and who gets to leave."

Nadine caught the worried expression on Angela's face. "What is it?"

"These dragons have been protected for hundreds of years. They have no protective or defensive instincts. They won't be able to survive in the wild if they grow larger than they already are."

"What about their natural instincts?"

"I really don't know," Angela sadly admitted. "They've been pampered, in terms of dragons, for too many generations."

"Generations?"

Angela scanned the various colors darting around them. "There are at least four original mating pairs…"

"Four pairs?" Nadine questioned. "But you previously said that there was only room for one fully grown dragon at the castle. How were there eight here at the time of the curse?"

Angela pulled back at Nadine's question. "I really don't know," she finally stammered out.

"How far up does the barrier go?" was Nadine's next question.

"What?" Angela blinked, wondering why she hadn't considered that question before.

"The barrier that froze everything in time. How big it is?"

"Why?" She couldn't understand why it really mattered when they were stuck within the estate boundaries regardless.

"What if the dragons were passing over and it triggered the curse on them?"

"Then why are they so small?"

"It was only a theory," Nadine snapped louder than she intended, briefly wondering if she needed to go inside and eat something.

Suddenly the dragons darted away, flying into the trees and up into their tower. Looking behind them, the girls saw Richmond standing underneath the archway that led into the garden. "That is why I never brought you out here," he commented. "When I was a boy, before I started changing, I would spend hours out here with these dragons."

"Where did they come from?" Angela asked.

"They used to fly over all the time before the curse took effect," he explained. "I would go exploring with…" he hesitated to finish, knowing it wasn't his story to tell. He couldn't even mention it if he wanted to. "With my father. He would show us all of the best dragon egg-laying places in the woods."

If the girls noticed Richmond's odd use of pronouns, they said nothing. They'd realized enough of the curse to understand that there were some things he simply could not talk about.

"How did they end up here?" Nadine nudged him for more answers.

"When the curse hit, I noticed that the normal-sized dragons were not returning to their nests. I collected all of the dragon eggs that I could get to that were on the grounds. There were about twelve eggs. I put them all in the kitchen behind the stove and wrapped them up in blankets. Eight of them hatched; they are the original eight miniature dragons."

Richmond started to laugh. "Thirteen years ago the age freezing part of the curse no longer impacted the visible living things, primarily impacting the dragons and me. They started breeding like crazy."

"Then why are they all the same size?" Nadine asked him. "Wouldn't the following generations grow bigger?"

"Not necessarily," Angela laughed. "Their DNA might have changed with the curse. We won't know if they'll remain this size until after the curse is broken."

"I wonder why it didn't impact the servants," Nadine mused, her thoughts shifting from dragons and back to the various impacts brought on by the curse.

"Because the servants are under a different curse," Angela supplied. "They are protected just in case Richmond lost his mind and went on a rampage."

"I have never…"

"I never said you did. I said in case you ever did. Some of your storyline, however, has gone insane while waiting for…" she turned and looked at Nadine.

"It's fine," Nadine smiled. "I understand."

However, Richmond's brows narrowed in confusion. "Some of my line has gone insane?"

"That's why there's always a…" Angela raised her hand to her throat, wondering why she couldn't finish her sentence.

"Always a what?" Nadine asked, looking back and forth between Angela and Richmond.

"The curse," Richmond replied, eyeing Angela as she continued to struggle to speak. "It won't let us talk about… it." When she still tried, he added, "And it won't let you speak until you drop it."

Choking out a cough, Angela sputtered, "That really hurts."

"I know."

Nadine narrowed her eyes at the pair. There was something that she didn't know and couldn't ask about; maybe she would look and see if the genealogy book could give her answers.

Chapter 17

Little Dragons

Slipping into the dragon tower, Nadine looked at the destruction that the little claws had created. Her research had let her down and she needed a break from staring at the tiny printed letters and words that had started floating around on the page.

"Wow!" she breathed, taking in the sight in front of her.

Over half of the dragons were curled up in piles that reminded her of piles of kittens. A few were nestled up on the rafters, a single open eye watching her as she examined the room. Noticing a shredded curtain on the opposite side of the open window, she carefully swept aside the panels and discovered the window that had been hidden.

Drawing in a breath, she stared, stunned, at the view around the castle from this window. There was a mountain range in the distance and she could see normal-sized dragons soaring through the skies. "Oh wow," she sighed.

Angela popped her head in the doorway, "I thought I would find you here when you weren't in the library."

"This view is amazing," she whispered, careful not to disturb the dragons that were sleeping.

"That direction is the Kingdom of Frosch Erbsen," Angela pointed out. "They have a deal with the Dragon Kingdom of Balaur."

Nadine cocked her head in thought, "German…" Nodding her head, she added, "That makes sense. A lot of fairy tales originated in Germany." She hesitated a moment, "For some reason, my father insisted that I learn German. I guess that makes sense now. Except…"

"Except what?"

"Frogs and Peas?"

Angela laughed for a moment before covering her mouth with a hand and looking around to see if she had disturbed the dragons.

After nothing moved, she returned to a whisper. "They are the kingdom for the Frog Prince and Princess and the Pea tales."

"Frogs and Peas," Nadine understood, nodding her head as if she was a bobblehead.

"In fact," Angela started to inform her, "many of these dragons are ancestors of those dragons you see flying around outside right now."

"Really?"

"Of course. Frosch Erbsen has that deal with the dragons," Angela repeated. The dragons protect their princesses while the Questers tackle their three quests."

"Where do the frogs and the peas come in?"

"Whenever there is a prince, his potential princess does have to go through the pea test along with two other tests. The frogs are merely figurative frogs, but we both know that saying about kissing a bunch of frogs before you find your prince."

Nadine took a step backward at Angela's words, letting go of the curtain as she moved. Most of the room darkened again, blocking the view of the neighboring kingdom. "Can they see us?"

"No," Angela replied. "As long as this curse lasts, all the other kingdoms see is either fog or their vision is redirected. The roads and paths redirect around the kingdom, except to enter a few of the outlying towns." Shaking her head, she asked, "Hasn't Richmond told you any of this stuff?"

"He probably has," Nadine admitted. "But everything was so textbook; this view, however, makes it all so real."

"If you look out the other window you should be able to see parts of Majstro, but not the ocean where the mermaids live. Just more and more trees," Angela pointed out, walking Nadine over to the other window.

"Oh my," Nadine barely breathed out. Then something clearly within the bounds of Oublié caught her attention. "Is that Rapunzel's tower?"

"Yes," Angela nodded. "It's right next to the boundary line. Nobody except the person intended to break that curse can enter the bewitched tower."

"But I can clearly see it," she pointed out.

"The Enchanted Forest does weave its roads around the tower, teasing people and attempting to draw Questers to its walls. Questers help fuel that curse's power, but thankfully those Questers don't die, usually. It depends on which enchantress is fueling the spells. However, the Rapunzel Cursed has to wait for its brother's curse to end." Angela jerked back in surprise when she realized how much she'd revealed.

"Brother's curse?" Nadine stared at that tower, feeling drawn to it for some unexplainable reason.

"The Rapunzel line has interconnected with Richmond's line, the Charmante line, and the Roschen line. Whenever one of those tales needs a sleeping prince or princess a tower will appear." Angela felt the curse preventing her from saying anything more detailed than that.

Nodding her head, Nadine accepted what Angela said without too much thought. "Makes sense to hide a sleeping princess in a forgotten kingdom."

"Right," Angela finally agreed after struggling to say more after several unsuccessful attempts.

Nadine was distracted enough to miss Angela's tone; normally she would recognize that her friend's single word carried the weight of what she couldn't say. Instead, she started watching a trio of dragons tumbling around and playing only as small dragons - or kittens - could.

"They are so cute."

"I know they might not look like it, but they are nothing like kittens."

Narrowing her eyes in concern, Nadine asked, "How did you know I was comparing them to kittens in my head?"

Laughing, "It was obvious. You had your, 'I want to stop and pet the kittens at the pet store' look." Angela had seen that look countless times when the girls had been taking a break near the pet store closest to the bakery.

"I don't have a kitten look."

"You most certainly do," Angela countered. "But these little dragons can shred you apart much easier than a cat. I'd hate to see what they can do if they wanted to inflict real damage to somebody or something."

"Richmond?" she whispered.

"They know he's unnatural. They know his outward appearance doesn't smell like his inner self. I believe that both the dragons and Richmond keep their distance from each other, especially after Richmond started to change," Angela wandered over to the window that overlooked Frosch Erbsen. She knew too much about that Rapunzel Tower to keep staring at it. Eventually, Nadine would notice the expressions that would undoubtedly inform her that Angela knew more than she was sharing.

"That must be horrible."

"Princess!" Angela snapped at Nadine as she turned just in time to watch her friend inch closer and closer to a napping dragon.

Jerking upright, Nadine flinched at her title. It was the first time she had heard it outside of the occasional playful occurrence between Richmond and herself. "Is calling me by my title really necessary?"

"You must get used to it."

"Richmond doesn't call me Princess unless he's teasing me."

"Richmond is a prince in his own right. You are of equal titles," Angela explained. "And once this curse is over and he marries, then he will be King Richmond, His Royal Highness to the Kingdom of Oublié. And you will be..."

Shaking her head, Nadine began to back up, mindful of the dragons scattered between her and the door. "No," she whispered. "No. I am no Queen. I am not fit to be a Queen. I don't have the training to be a Queen. A librarian maybe. Definitely a middle school English teacher. A small-town bakery owner is not far from the realm of possibility..."

"The Tradition," Angela started to interrupt Nadine's rambling.

"Hang the Tradition!" Nadine shouted. "All because of some Tradition I'm being forced to marry somebody. I have no free will. I have no choices. I entered a garden when I was eight and some faceless magical force decided that I was the right person to break a curse. I was eight!"

Angela was surprised that it had taken Nadine this long to break down over the inevitability of her situation. She was also stunned that the dragons were merely sitting up, staring at the distressed princess. Even the ones that had been playing had landed and were facing Nadine.

"Why haven't they attacked me?" she whispered, feeling calmer after her outburst. Now she was worried at the way every single miniature dragon was staring at her.

"I don't know," Angela replied.

"Because," a grumbly voice that had been hiding in the hallway answered, "they know that you don't mean them any harm." Moments later, he disappeared down the short corridor.

Turning around, Nadine shrieked, "Richmond!" Darting through the doorway, she let out a string of curse words when she realized that he was over halfway down the spiral staircase. Spinning to face Angela, she asked, "Do you think she heard my outburst?"

All Angela could do was sadly nod yes.

Chapter 18

Intent

Richmond didn't appear for dinner later that night. The girls silently ate, each lost in their own thoughts. Nadine was worried about Richmond. Angela started to strategize for what she expected to happen soon.

Looking up, she broke the silence and asked, "How many quests have you had?"

Shaking her head, Nadine looked up, "I don't know."

"You don't know?"

"It's not like I'm going to know what my quests are until after they happen. Or that I'll have to save Richmond from the tiny dragons…"

Angela groaned as she anticipated what was bound to happen next.

"What?" Nadine asked with her fork paused halfway to her mouth.

"You just tempted fate, or the Tradition," Angela answered her.

It took Nadine five hours to find Richmond. She had started yawning over an hour ago, but she suspected that she wouldn't be able to go to sleep without apologizing to Richmond. She didn't mean her outburst the way it seemed, but she was fighting against the knowledge that everything had been taken out of her hands.

Finally, she found him calmly sitting in the middle of the little dragon tower. "Is this safe?"

He merely shrugged.

Keeping a careful eye on the dragons that were curled up and sleeping around the room, Nadine cautiously made her way around them until she could sit down next to Richmond. Once there she noticed that there was a dragon curled up in his lap and another burrowed in the hair around his neck.

This dragon, the one disturbed when Richmond had shrugged, sleepily opened one eye and studied Nadine before going back to sleep.

"What's the matter?" she whispered, watching his eyes as he looked around the room and didn't say anything. "Of course. If you say anything, you'll disturb them. You can't even move right now."

They sat there, silently making eye contact for nearly five minutes. Nadine wanted to squirm nervously and look away several times. Instead, she found herself leaning forward, placing her hands around Richmond's lap to stabilize her, and giving him a quick kiss.

The incisors felt a little odd against her lips, but she didn't care. She raised herself up a little more, placing her hands on his thighs this time instead of the floor, to place another kiss on his forehead and nose.

Pulling back, she softly explained, "I don't like what the Tradition forces the royals to do. You have been stuck here, by yourself, for way too long. Who knows what happens to others. I read that my mother had to face a were-huntsman that had been killing girls wearing red-hooded cloaks. Some princes and princesses have to sleep in towers for hundreds of years until somebody that they have never met before rescues them."

She closed her eyes for a moment to gather her thoughts.

While Nadine was thinking, Richmond watched her carefully. He had been terrified of what she would say as soon as she found him, but this was going better than expected. It was difficult to resist the urge to cup her face with one of his claws after she had kissed him.

"I'm angry at the Tradition, but not with you," she finally whispered. "If that Tradition hadn't been pushing my life in the direction it needed to go for this tale, my adoptive parents would still be alive. I never would have left my biological parents. I would have had sisters and a brother who could have loved me, and now our relationships are most likely going to be awkward."

Opening her eyes, she looked at Richmond again. Concluding, Nadine smiled at him, "But I can't fully regret the Tradition pushing us together. It probably saw something in us that told it that I could break this curse on you, even when I was eight. Any of my sisters could have been forced into this situation, but I was and that probably was for a reason. I cannot regret meeting you and while I don't love you right now, I know that I can and will someday."

The burst of power that exploded at Nadine's words startled the dragons, causing them to jump into action. While miniature dragons darted and dashed around the room, Richmond pushed Nadine back, covering her body from the frenzied activities of startled dragons.

"Don't move," he mumbled, tucking his head down as he held himself over her.

Arms braced around her, his massive size blocking her vision, Nadine tightly closed her eyes. "What's going on?"

Only Richmond couldn't answer her. The glow surrounding them blinded him and he'd closed his eyes. But he could feel his teeth returning to their normal sizes. The horns on his head disappeared. His claws returned to hands. All of the fur, and every other animalistic feature that marked him as cursed, disappeared.

Finally, the dragons settled down and Richmond rolled off Nadine. "It's safe now," a voice reached her ears, only slightly similar to the deeper bass that Richmond normally addressed her with.

"Richmond?" she asked, sitting upright and staring at the normal male in oversized clothes who had nearly collapsed next to her. Chocolate brown eyes opened, eyes she could never forget after their silent bonding moment not that long ago.

Sitting up, Richmond found himself unsteady. It was made worse when Nadine launched herself at him, wrapping her arms around his neck and slamming her lips against his.

This time it felt different without any teeth pressing against her. This time Richmond was able to kiss her back.

They would have lost track of time if it hadn't been for Angela clearing her throat from the doorway. "It looks as if you both have gone through all three of your quests."

"How is that possible?" Nadine asked, pulling away from Richmond.

He paid more attention to the flush that was painting Nadine's cheeks than Angela in the doorway.

Angela held up a finger with each quest she listed off, "You managed to find your way back to the manor, discovered your heritage by asking for help, and you accepted the Tradition even though you admitted that you were annoyed by it."

"And me?" Richmond asked. "I'm human again, but I don't think I completed my three trials."

Breathing the air, Angela examined the magic surrounding Richmond. "No, you haven't," she admitted. "You still have one quest left."

"Then why am I human?"

"Because Nadine loves you."

"I didn't say that," Nadine protested.

"I heard what you said," Angela interrupted before either of them could argue any further. "You have been hurt before by my brother and you need a little more time to emotionally recover, but the Tradition accepts that you know that you will love Richmond given more time. It doesn't need you to fall head over heels in love at first sight or any of that other nonsense. Even the Tradition understands that sometimes the best love stories are when friends gradually fall in love."

She then turned to Richmond and added, "And that can't happen until you complete your third quest."

"What were my quests?" Richmond asked because he was confused. He couldn't figure it out.

"You realized that even your servants were people and you just protected Nadine from the dragons. They could have done some serious damage to both of you as you were transforming. In fact, protecting her with your body managed to create a magical barrier that kept the dragons out."

Looking around the room, Nadine noticed something. "Where are the dragons?"

Nodding her head, Angela explained. "As soon as the curse was broken, somebody was able to enter the gates without Richmond having to let them in. They are currently holding him hostage."

"Guy," Nadine breathed.

"Unfortunately," Angela confirmed. Turning towards Richmond, she added, "I think this is your last quest and I think the Tradition wants you to handle this one as a human and not as a dangerous beast. It might be why it transformed you back when it did."

Wrinkles formed between Nadine's brows as she considered what her friend was saying. It took a minute for her to understand that while fairy tales had their own rules, sometimes magic had to bend and break them in order to complete the tale.

Nodding her head, Angela raised her arm over her head and twirled. A moment later, she had disappeared. Nadine and Richmond would have to take the stairs.

Chapter 19

When Guy wandered into the garden, he didn't expect the bombardment. Out of nowhere, over fifty miniature dragons dive-bombed him. Raising his arms over his head, he felt the tiny pricks of their claws digging into his flesh.

Letting out a string of curses, Guy dropped to the ground in the hope that the dragons would go away. Instead, they landed on him and settled down into a jumbled ball of dragons. Some curled up in a pile on his back, tails twitching. One or two of them sat on his head and neck. Three settled in front of him, facing his head as they observed him carefully. He watched them back, eyes huge and wary. Guy had no clue that there were three more on the other side of his head and three more at the top of his head.

About twenty dragons had gathered on his legs, climbing and clawing over him. The rest flew around him, darting around enough to keep him from being able to get up. If he could get through the thirty dragons that were on him or around his head, he would still have to get through the ten more dragons that were flying over him, some which were dive-bombing every time they noticed an opening.

With a flash of blue light, Angela appeared. Shooing the flying dragons away, she greeted her older brother, "Hello, Gaubert."

"It's Guy."

"No," she shook her head. "It's Gaubert. Just like I can't escape the name Mother gave me, Angelique."

"What is this about?" he hissed, drawing back when a dragon hissed at him.

"Why are you even here?" Angela asked, ignoring his question.

"Why do you think I'm here?"

"I think you want to follow in Mother's crooked footsteps and destroy the Enchanted Forest."

He let out a harsh laugh. "You couldn't be any more right," Guy snarled from where he was detained.

"I just can't figure out why," she stated, stalling long enough for Richmond and Nadine to join them. "Why would you want to destroy your own existence? Why are you out to destroy Richmond and Nadine?"

Snorting, Guy would have rolled his eyes if he hadn't been face down on the garden's cobblestone pathway. "The last question is easy. In order to take down the Forest, I have to take out one of the fairy tale pairs. What better pairing to destroy than the Forgotten Prince and his beautiful bride. I'd hoped she would fall for my charms and, much like her stepsister, into my bed. That would be one way to destroy the tale."

Angela resisted the urge to roll her eyes. A heroine's virginity was not a be-all-end-all as it would have once been. Too many fairy tale princesses that went off to be fostered did not return as innocent as when they had left the Forest.

"If I could have killed her there I would have," Guy continued. "Regrettably, that was not an option. But if a horrible beast attacked me and I killed him in self-defense, and if the princess held captive had already gone insane and jumped out of a tower, well…" he drawled with a sickening and sinister smirk, "…that would not be my fault."

"But…" Angela started to interrupt before deciding not to point out one of the critical facts that her brother had overlooked - the Tradition had a built-in backup plan. There was also the part where he had been able to climb a wall that had previously been magically protected against intruders.

"The best part," he added, not noticing that his sister had started to interrupt, "is that nobody will ever miss them because nobody even remembers that Richmond exists. This entire kingdom has been forgotten."

Laughter from the garden's entrance drew his attention. Several of the dragons sat up, claws digging into his back. Drawing in a breath, Guy was more nervous about the dragon around his neck than he previously had been.

Although the dragon still curled up on his spinal cord was unnerving.

And the dragons sitting on his ankles could do some serious damage to some tendons.

"I wish I could say that it was a pleasure to see you again, Guy," Nadine greeted him. "However, if you hadn't stolen my book of fairy tales I never would have returned here, so I guess you do deserve some credit for my current happiness."

Secretly, Nadine was pleased to see the blood flowing from his back thanks to the little dragon claws still piercing him. He didn't have to manipulate Meg or lie to them; simple breaking and entering while she was at work would have sufficed.

"There's also one more thing," Richmond stated, taking a step forward and out of the shadows where he was concealing his physical changes. Coldly, he watched Gaubert - he would always be Gaubert to him - and the little dragons surrounding him. Even he noticed the one that was curled up dangerously close to the veins in Gaubert's neck.

"What is that?" he hissed, mindless towards the dragons. He had begun to notice that Richmond was no longer a beast.

"Since I am no longer a beast, the kingdom is no longer forgotten," Richmond calmly stated. "Gaubert…"

Interrupting, he hissed, "Guy. It's Guy."

Enunciating, "Gaubert," Richmond continued. "As soon as the curse broke, Nadine's mother, the Queen of Wonderland, became aware of where her daughter is located. I wouldn't be surprised if her parents soon appeared on the other side of the gates."

Angela added, "You spent days trying to find a way into this estate. What made you think the curse still existed once you were able to scale the fence?"

At her words, Richmond froze. Turning to Nadine, he hissed, "Go to the gates. Do not let your parents cross over the boundary onto the estate."

"What?" Nadine asked, shaking her head in confusion. "Why?"

"Because the curse isn't completely broken," he admitted. "I'll explain later."

Once she had taken off towards the gates as at a sprint, Richmond turned back to Angela. "We still can't leave. You know why."

"Right," she nodded her head. "What are we going to do about him?"

"Hey!" Guy shouted from his place on the ground. "I'm right here."

"He'll magic himself out of my dungeons and we can't ask the dragons to constantly sit on him until the second part of the curse is broken."

"And I can't magically bind him," Angela admitted. "As soon as he's free he's only going to go around killing every living thing on the grounds, including these dragons."

"And I'm fairly certain my servants are no longer invisible," Richmond pointed out. Turning to Gaubert, he asked, "Why do you want my estate?"

"There are magical reserves underneath your land," he admitted, seeing no reason not to tell them. All it would take would be a single word and they could have the dragons shred him to pieces.

Letting out a burst of laughter that had caught a few more dragons' attention and caused Guy to clinch with panic, Richmond started to shake his head. "There are no magical reserves underneath my estate," he laughed. "The Enchanted Forest stores its power within the untamed parts of the forest. That's why paths can change and horrors like deadly dragons and werewolves exist."

Angela added, "And, unlike Mother's teachings, killing off the Tradition's pawns only causes the fairy tales to no longer exist. Without the tales, the Forest and the Tradition does not exist. Without them there is no magic."

The remaining blood in Guy's face disappeared. Suddenly he seemed smaller than before as everything he believed was torn from him. "And without magic..."

"We become human or no longer exist," Angela finished for him.

He no longer had nothing to lose, but he also had nothing to gain.

With a single hand, the dragons were dismissed. Even though they weren't needed any longer, a handful of them settled in as an improvised guard surrounding Guy.

Sitting up, he felt Angela healing the wounds on his back. "Mother is going to kill me," he mumbled.

"She was going to kill you regardless," Angela dryly stated. "She tried to kill me and steal all of my power, but that is a story for another time."

Chapter 20

Family Reunion

At the gates, Nadine stood watching and waiting. Suddenly a guard wearing a uniform that reminded her of a deck of cards appeared out of the trunk of a tree.

"Princess Nadine?" the Spade asked, trying to shake off the effects that traveling through portals had on his head.

"And you are?"

"I was assigned as your Tracker and Bodyguard when you were sent off to live with your Foster Parents. Your birth mother, Queen Gabrielle of Wonderland and her husband, King Ethan, sent me ahead of them to make certain that everything was going according to plan."

"According to plan?" she half asked, half snorted. "I have been instructed to keep anybody from crossing over that boundary," she pointed at the gates, "and onto these grounds. Anybody who enters cannot leave."

Nodding his head, the Spade admitted that this was a complication. "I'll be back with your parents," he finally said, turning to leave back through the tree.

"Wait!" Nadine called back. "What is your name?"

"Sawyer," he grinned. "I happen to be the third of my siblings, like you are." Pausing for a moment, he added, "And I am also one of your cousins." With a nod of his head, he walked right into the trunk of a tree and disappeared.

Taking a deep breath, Nadine steeled herself for what she now knew was about to happen. She was about to meet her parents. Possibly her siblings. Maybe even a few more cousins and an aunt and uncle or two.

Something behind her caught her attention. Richmond, followed by Angela, stalked towards him. "What's going on? Where's Guy?"

Rolling her eyes, Angela answered her. "Gaubert is currently being guarded by the dragons in the garden. He is well aware that if he makes one threatening move that one of the dragons, probably the one curled up around his neck, is likely to attack."

They didn't have to wait long for Sawyer to reemerge from the portal hidden in the tree. Moments later The Queen of Wonderland and her husband walked through, hand in hand. Following them was a clone of the Queen; she could only be Nadine's oldest sister, Alice.

Looking back and forth between her parents, she cataloged the similarities between them. While Alice had that traditional fairy tale blonde hair, Nadine noticed that her hair was a slightly darker blonde than her sister's was. She suspected it was thanks to her father's dark brown hair genes; it made sense why, before entering the Enchanted Forest, her hair was a light brown shade.

"Where's Grace?" was the first thing Nadine squeaked out.

Queen Gabrielle and King Ethan looked at each other.

"You remember Grace?" the Queen asked.

"Richmond's library had a genealogy book. We researched my family tree weeks ago," Nadine answered her, nervously. "I needed to know." Feeling nerves she never really felt before, not even when she stood on stage and gave her graduation commencement speech in high school, she bit the left side of her bottom lip. Looking down, it started to hit her that her mother was within touching distance and she couldn't cross that border.

To make matters even worse, Alice was glaring at her. "Grace went off looking for you as soon as we figured out that you were in this kingdom."

"And Charlie?"

"Went looking for Grace when she didn't return after a few weeks." Then Alice turned to glare at Richmond. "Why don't you tell us where Grace is? And why you can't cross over the estate boundary?"

Richmond looked directly at Alice for a long moment. Finally, after drawing in a deep breath, he turned to address Nadine. "I have a younger brother. As soon as Mum and Dad died and the curse hit at the very beginning, before you had even wandered into my garden the first time…"

"The first time?" Queen Gabrielle questioned.

"Long story," Nadine replied. "So, you have a younger brother. Where is he?"

They watched the various expressions pass over his face. Confusion. Sadness. Longing. Anger.

"We have a Sleeping Beauty in our family line. And a Rapunzel. Somewhere in this kingdom is a tower…"

The King and Queen looked at each other in shock. "Round white tower over fifty feet tall?"

"Yes?" he answered them, the question in his voice.

"We wandered into a massive tower when we were going through my quests in the Enchanted Forest before I returned to Wonderland," Queen Gabrielle answered him. "Only there was no door."

"There wouldn't be if you weren't the person meant to enter the tower."

This time the King spoke up, "So which tale is my middle daughter currently in?"

"I don't have a clue."

Also Available by this Author:

Standalones
The Secrets Between Us

The Magic Chronicles
Half-Moon Manor (Olivia and Henry's Story)
Keeping Secrets

The Hastings Sisters Novels
The Consequences of Being Aiden (Ainsley's story)
The Trouble with Chasing Aileen
The Problem with Finding Ashlynn
Untitled Aiden's Story (Coming Soon)

The Enchanted Forest
Into the Enchanted Forest
The Cursed Garden
The Bewitched Tower (Coming Soon)
The Runaway Princess (Coming Soon)
The Princess and the Dragon (Coming Soon)
Ander and the Cocky Dragon Slayer

The Bookworm Next Door Series
Stephanie Makes the Match
The Party
The Bookworm's Makeover
The Bookworm Next Door
Along the Road
Near the Finish Line

The Summer After Graduation
The Bookworm Next Door: The High School Stories
  Collection

The Jane Austen Variations
Persuaded (Persuasion)
First Impressions (Coming Soon)

About the Author

Alicia Chumney has her B.A. in English Literature and her 7-12 English teacher certification. Since middle school, she has been scribbling in notebooks, on scrap paper, even in a restaurant ticket book one time (she still has the ticket book).

She lives in Tennessee with her cat, Molly, and a stack of books that she doubts she will finish reading in her lifetime. This is mostly because she spends a fair amount of time rereading her favorite books: Anne of Green Gables and Pride and Prejudice.

You can find her on:

Facebook

Twitter

Goodreads

Made in the USA
Columbia, SC
04 November 2020